THE WHITE CHIP

A Western Story

THE WHITE CHIP

A Western Story

by Nelson C. Nye

Five Star Western
Thorndike, Maine

A Five Star Western published in conjunction with Golden West Literary Agency.

February 1996

First Edition

Five Star Standard Print Western Series.

The text of this edition is unabridged.

Set in 11 pt. News Plantin by Jason Johnson.

Printed in the United States on permanent paper.

Library of Congress Cataloging in Publication Data

Nye, Nelson C. (Nelson Coral), 1907–
    The white chip : a western story / Nelson C. Nye.
— 1st ed.
        p.   cm.
    ISBN 0-7862-0565-2 (hc)
    I. Title.
    PS3527.Y33W45   1996
    813'.54—dc20   95-40636

Foreword

The two most celebrated and searched for bonanzas in the entire Southwest are the Lost Dutchman mine and Breyfogle's ledge, the first in the Superstition Mountains of central Arizona, the other in Death Valley. Both were lost in the 1800s; both have been sought by hundreds of persons over the intervening years — prospectors, soldiers, cowhands, mining men, adventurers, and plain damn' fools too avid to count the cost.

We are looking here for the source of the Dutchman's gold. Long before Jacob Walzer was heard of, rumors of gold in the Superstitions had lured many others into those dreadful mountains. Not all who braved this rugged desolation returned to tell of it. I've been there myself, on one occasion in the company of Walzer's niece.

Most searchers during the past eighty years were well aware of the dangers, but neither risks nor restrictions have proven sufficient to deter men in the throes of gold fever and the rose-colored dreams of immeasurable wealth.

One group of seven — six men and a girl — are the searchers this story is all about.

Nelson C. Nye
Tucson, 1995

Chapter One

GIRL WITH A MAP

We were in the back room of the Arizona Club on the fringe of Tucson's Mexican quarter — Spartokori, Cookson, Butch Schroeder, Quintada, and myself. The cards were forgotten in startled reaction to the deal Ebbert Snude had just dumped in our laps.

Spartokori, with a thriving business in collectors' items, disgustedly peering past the smoke dribbling up from the hand-rolled dangling from a pendulous lower lip was first to speak.

"You got to be plumb out of your skull if you're seriously proposing to go into those mountains on a hunt for that crazy Dutchman's mine!"

I saw the amusement in Snude's cat-sly glance. He'd been called some rather nasty things since he'd assumed the presidency of Beach & Bascomb's Commercial Bank, but with all his clout could not have cared less for other folks' opinions. Well into his sixties and hard as nails, he was a tough-minded relic of the Tucson Ring and tighter than a boar's ass, which made his present proposal little short of extraordinary in the light of his offer to stand good for the bulk of our expenses.

"It's there," he said. "Whenever Walzer ran short of cash, he went into those mountains and came out with gold ore. . . ."

"You don't know that," Bob Cookson declared. "All any of us know is nothing but hearsay, handed down and enlarged by wishful thinking."

"There's no hearsay," Snude smiled, "about that check for

two hundred and fifty thousand dollars he cashed at my bank. That check came from the mint. For the burro loads of jewelry rock he's known to have shipped them. You're a hard-headed business man, Bob, but facts is facts. That ore came out of the Superstitions. Any number of persons saw him and his loaded burros coming out of there. A flock of people saw and handled chunks of that rock. . . ."

"And thousands more," Butch Schroeder grumbled, "went in there lookin' for it and come out empty-handed . . . those that come out," he added with a scowl.

Snude said imperturbably, "I admit the risks, but with seven of us, sticking together and all well armed, I consider those risks reduced to a worthwhile gamble."

It was Quintada who voiced the next objection. "Why do you want that Peralta girl with us? Looks like to me. . . ."

"The girl has a map."

Considering the thoughtful looks this brought out, I said, "You think she's related to the last of the Peraltas supposed to have had mines in those mountains? You think the Dutchman's gold came from one of those mines?"

Snude nodded, but Cookson said without concealing his contempt, "Maps are a dime a dozen around here."

Snude said patiently, "In view of the old Spanish *arrastras* that have been discovered, there's no doubt in my mind the Peraltas had mines in that area before the Apaches came down on them. Everyone knows how the Apaches regarded those mountains. So long as only a few palefaces were gophering around the Indians put up with them. It was only when the Peraltas fetched in a lot of helpers that the redmen dug up the hatchet and went on the warpath. It was at the Peraltas' base camp . . . since called the Massacre Grounds . . . that Silverlock and Goldlock later recovered more than fifteen thousand dollars worth of gold."

"But the Massacre Grounds are above and east of Goldfield,"

Schroeder objected. "I thought the Peraltas were supposed to have come into the mountains by what's now called the Peralta Road that goes into Boulder Cañon."

"And comes out," Snude smiled, "below Black Mesa which isn't more than a whoop and a holler from that camp you just mentioned. They had other camps in the Superstitions. They had one just east of Tortilla Mountain." With his bright little eyes rummaging our faces, he continued, "No point hashing over all this past history. I've seen the girl's map and it certainly has the look of something old man Peralta might well have drawn."

"If you've seen the map," Bob Cookson asked, "why bring the girl into this?"

"She gave me no time to study the thing, only gave me a quick look at it when she came to me suggesting I get up a party to go after the rest of it. The map was her proof of being related to the right branch of the Peralta family. She claims Jacob Walzer's gold came from one of their mines and has a chunk of the Peralta ore she says she got from her Uncle Gonzales along with the map."

"And she's positive, of course," Quintada said skeptically, "the map will show where the Dutchman dug out his gold."

"No, she doesn't think that. All the map shows, she says, is the location of those old Peralta claims."

"And it's a cinch," Cookson said, "you didn't see enough of it to know where they're at. I doubt that map's worth the paper it's drawn on."

"Nobody's forcing you to join this hunt," Snude pointed out. "If you fellers aren't interested, I won't have any trouble finding people who'll be only too happy to go out there with me. A bonanza of this magnitude. . . ."

"Is just another pipe dream," Butch Schroeder growled.

"Walzer," I said, "was a mining engineer. If he hadn't figured there was gold in those mountains, he'd never have gone in there."

Spartokori's glance jumped around to have another look at me. "You're a mining man, Brannigan. What do you think about Snude's proposal?"

"Well," I said, "Jake Walzer's gold was no pipe dream. That much I'm sure of. That it came from the Superstitions I'm also willing to gamble on, having talked some years ago with a couple of rannies who saw him come out of there with loaded burros. Whether it came from a mountain or one of those cañons is anybody's guess. That the source of Jake's gold has never been located doesn't prove it didn't come from there. I'll go along with Snude if he wants to outfit us."

"The deal," Snude said, "calls for each of you to put up two hundred dollars, cash on the barrelhead, for provisions and equipment. I'll take care of the transport, but you'll each have to furnish your own riding animals. And rifles."

"What about the girl?" Cookson asked.

Snude said with a grin, "She's putting up the map."

This brought out some more argument to which he listened with a hard-held patience. When they ran out of breath, he said, "Those who want in on this will now fork up the price of admission."

"I haven't got two hundred dollars," Quintada said angrily.

"Then you've got exactly four days to find it. We'll be leaving here on the fifth," the banker said, "bright and early. There's others, I reckon, will be glad to take your place."

Fishing in his pocket Snude dropped on the table between us a small piece of rock about the size of a hen's egg that appeared to be about eighty percent gold. "This," he informed us, "is a piece of the Dutchman's ore. And this" — producing a second and somewhat larger chunk — "we have on loan from the girl who was given it by her uncle along with the map. According to what Gonzales told her, it came from one of those

10

Peralta mines."

He gave a sly cackle at the expressions he saw on our staring faces. The samples weren't as alike as two peas in a pod, but for color and content you couldn't help believing they'd come from the same ground. Except for size and shape they appeared identical, a powerful argument in favor of this project. But I did not care much for the look with which he probed those avid faces. Too much the expression of a stalking cat.

"Well?" he said abruptly. "You in this or aren't you? If not," he said, taking a squint at his watch, "I'm catching the next stage north."

Always willing to take a gamble I was first to put my money on the table. One by one the others followed suit, all but Quintada who was eyeing us resentfully. Grimacing he finally said, "Count me in. I'll get the money."

Looking back on our monthly poker sessions, it wasn't hard to understand why Schroeder and myself had been offered shares in this venture. Obviously Snude figured to go in there with a large enough party to make interference appear too costly. The two hundred dollars a head, I guessed, was mostly a ploy to rule Quintada out. Once the word got out, it would be no problem to replace any of us. And Quintada, if not included, would almost certainly shoot off his mouth.

Butch Schroeder, a butcher by trade, was known to be a crack shot with pistol or rifle, the kind of galoot you'd want on your side in the event of trouble. Aside from the monthly poker games I knew very little about him, but he had, I thought, an inquiring mind.

It was easy to see why I'd been included, having worked several years as a hand on the Tortilla Ranch in the Superstition country between Black Cross Butte and Tortilla Mountain. I was known to have explored most of the cañons and several of the mountains, though mostly just looking and digging a little in places that

11

seemed likely. That I hadn't found anything made no difference to Snude; what he wanted from me was my knowledge of the layout, for this was a region it was easy to get lost in. Quite a number of people had, and some had been murdered. It had some breathtaking views and a bad reputation.

Bob Cookson was a skeptical hard-headed business man who dealt in anything he figured would make a profit. Quintada had some kind of a horse ranch south of town off the road to Tubac and the Mexican border. A lean, wiry *hombre* who had the look of one whose mother had worn moccasins, a persistent rumor had him tied in with smugglers, though what they smuggled was still an open question. I imagined it was rifles to arm Mexican *bandidos*. With that scraggly mustache and beetling brows, he might easily have been taken for a bandit himself.

Snude shoved back his chair and, apparently having second thoughts about Quintada, said, "Tell you what I'll do, Pepe. I want a dozen good stout mules for this trip. If you can come up with them, keep the price within reason, and take charge of them for us, I'll buy them from you."

So maybe I was wrong about that two hundred smackers we'd had to pony up. Perhaps it had nothing to do with Quintada and it had been Snude's intention all along to have him with us. In any event the fellow was earnestly bobbing his head, obsequious as a hat-in-hand peon.

"*¡Sí, sí, señor!* Where do you want them, and when?"

"Have them at the O. K. Corral at least one full day before we set off. I'll be wanting to look them over."

Cookson said, "Why mules, Eb? Thought it was burros the Dutchman used?"

Snude, digging up a smile for Bob, nodded. "That's right. It was. But mules, being bigger, can pack more gold when we're ready to come out of there. Isn't that right, Pepe?"

Quintada, bobbing and smirking like an organ-grinder's monkey, agreed. And why shouldn't he — with the price of mules on its way up again and one of his relatives no doubt raising them?

I wondered, why had the old Dutchman always used burros to pack his jewelry rock out of the mountains? And what sort of bee had Snude got in his bonnet to spur him into putting hard cash in this hunt for a legend he had scoffed at for years? Had he gone off his rocker for this Peralta filly? Or was it her map that was responsible for building a fire under him?

Chapter Two

THROUGH A KITCHEN WINDOW

With the others scarcely able to haul their stares off that pair of incredibly rich specimens glinting so enticingly beneath the Rochester lamp, I was a heap more concerned with what lay back of this. Though heartily disliked by a great many persons Ebbert Snude had not got where he was — one of the county's wealthiest men — by playing the fool. The sort to skin a flea for its hide and tallow, I suspicioned that he knew a lot more than he'd told.

Only two things was I able to think of which could have put him so suddenly into a sweat to track down a mine that to my way of thinking had never existed. Either the map or that female who had dug it up for him. Sure the Southwest was filled with tales of lost mines, and none so diligently sought as the one Jake Walzer was believed to have got his ore from. In the last forty years maps, as indicated by Cookson, had become a flourishing business — Peralta maps especially. I reckoned it had to be this girl that had put Snude's bowels in an uproar.

Schroeder said, "I think you ought to get an expert's opinion on the age of that paper. But even if it was drawn by old Miguel himself, he had to have done it before those quakes. So what good is it? That whole country was shook up. Any landmarks left would sure as hell have been altered."

With his glance seeking mine I nodded. "Sounds reasonable."

"Could have buried whole cañons."

"Well, parts of them anyway. And opened up others."

Cookson said, "Chuck's been all through there. If that map is the one drawn by Don Miguel for his family, Brannigan will know once he gets a good look at it if there's enough landmarks left for it to do us any good."

I said dubiously, "Maybe." At this point in time I'd no reason to tell them it wasn't mines I'd been hunting.

After picking his money that was left from the card playing up off the table, Schroeder, whose shop was in Globe, said he'd better be going and took himself off. Quintada, too, went out to get on his horse and head for the Nogales road. A few minutes later I said my good nights, leaving Cookson and Snude to settle up with the Arizona Club for the use of the room.

I'd come to Tombstone to take care of a bit of business I had with Johnny Behan and had been staying that week in Nellie Cashman's hotel over on Frémont Street, and had come up to Tucson mainly for this once-a-month poker game. As I rounded the first corner, I dropped a hand to my belt when a man stepped out of the heavier shadows which a sky full of stars did little to lighten. It wasn't till he spoke that I recognized Schroeder.

"No call for bullets. Just thought we oughta put our heads together," he tossed at me gruffly in a lowered voice.

"About Snude's proposal?"

"Yeah. Why's he countin' us in?"

"He'll have his reasons. He's not the sort to go in there solo. Expect he wants to make sure of getting out."

Schroeder snorted. "Think we'll find anything?"

"Wouldn't bet we won't."

"Give you odds," Schroeder grunted, "it won't be the Dutchman's mine."

"No," I said, "that talk about Jake was the sugar coating meant to suck us into this and that two hundred was just to make sure we wouldn't duck out should the deal come apart."

"That's my notion," Schroeder nodded. "He's after somethin'

15

chock full of risk or he'd never been cuttin' us peons in on it."

"Thinks he's got a hot lead on one of those Peralta mines, I reckon."

"Those ore samples both come out of the same hole, no two ways about that."

"Sure. A cache," I said. "Walzer was never into those mountains long enough to mine the ore he brought out. That gold was all of it right there waitin'."

"Gold, you reckon, the Peraltas dug up?"

"Possibly hidden by Apaches after rubbin' them out."

"Whatever," he said. "If anything's found, we'll be goddamned lucky to come out of there with it!"

"I been thinkin' about that. We damn' well better be keepin' our eyes skinned."

Nodding, Schroeder muttered, "Wouldn't trust that bugger any farther'n I could throw him . . . nor that Greek, either. Better figure to watch the both of them." Filling his mouth with tobacco, he chomped a while and spat. "Reckon I better head for Globe."

Without further talk he strode off into the shadows. Saddle leather screeched and a moment later I heard the sound of departing hoofs. Moving on, I mulled over the little I knew about him, which wasn't much. He had come into Globe a couple years back driving a rig for one of the freighters. Had quit his employer to open a butcher shop. That much I'd picked up here and there, word of mouth. A compulsive gambler who enjoyed playing cards and never spoke of himself. Long exposure to desert sun had given him the look of saddle-soaped leather, a country man's face, except for one thing — you could never be sure what lay back of that unblinking, slate-colored stare.

He appeared to be somewhere in his early forties. On the infrequent occasions I'd been in his company, I felt I was being studied though I'd never caught him at it. Nor had I previously

16

encountered a poker-faced butcher.

In case you're feeling curious about me, where I'd come from and why, I don't mind saying I'd migrated from Texas a long time ago, figuring I might get shut of things still carried in my head. It seemed like now I wouldn't ever forget them. When I came away from there, I was a pretty impressionable, long-legged kid, son of a feisty Irishman who'd had the unmitigated gall to squat on six hundred and forty acres of a big cowman's choice grass, bullheadedly ignoring all orders to move. I don't know what happened to my old man, but I can still hear the ground-shaking thunder of fast running horses.

It was the gunshots, I reckon, that jerked me from sleep to go padding through the dark to peer, heart pounding, through a kitchen window to discover my Mexican mother crumpled and lifeless on the porch steps and just beyond, in the lamplight spilling from the open door, the shape of a man crouched above a smoking pistol.

I guess in fifteen years people change considerably. I wasn't sure yet if that fellow was the butcher, but I couldn't help wondering . . . ? Back in my room at the Congress Hotel I got to sleep looking forward to finding out what that skinflint banker was up to and — a big maybe — learning if Schroeder was the fellow staring at my mother from behind that just-fired pistol.

Chapter Three

BOUND FOR THE SUPERSTITIONS

There wasn't much chance of keeping word from getting around once the six of us assembled at the O. K. Corral to pick up Quintada and the dozen pack mules. We got out of there while the stars still shone and the streets pretty much deserted, but we'd no way of muzzling the livery's help.

Snude, in puncher garb with a Winchester across his saddle-bow, rode up ahead with the last of the Peraltas, the packed mules next, and the rest of us eating their dust in the procession's tail end. Quite a sight, I reckoned, and a deal too much of one to my way of thinking. I suppose this was Snude's way of serving warning we were not to be trifled with.

Serafina Peralta, even in jeans and a man's cotton shirt with her chestnut curls tucked up out of sight in that chin-strapped sombrero, could not have been taken for a boy by anyone. Like the gray Barb she rode, breeding was evident from top to bootsoles. She was stunningly attractive with those high-boned, olive-skinned features, and her smiles were bright as the morning's sun.

It was very soon evident the banker had no intention of giving rise to speculation by taking our outfit near any towns. Once past the low hills in the dregs of the night, we were well into the desert, heading west before the stars were lost behind the pink spreading banners of the rising sun. A cool breeze was blowing through the sparse broom and cholla, but it didn't take long to have us out of our brush jackets.

By the middle of the morning, traveling cavalry fashion, we had crossed the north-flowing Santa Cruz gurgling down out of Mexico. It was well past noon when we skirted Tucson, keeping well south of the mission and still heading west. With the scattered adobes of Marana distantly visible to the left, we swung north into higher country with the brush-clad slopes of the Tortillas blue in the heat-hazed distance off to the right.

With these not yet left behind, it was past seven o'clock when we made a dry camp, stretched stiff legs, and unloaded the mules. It was going to be a cold night, but the banker said, "No fires! You don't know who may be on the lookout for us."

"What about supper?" Spartokori asked.

"We've plenty of jerky . . . chew some of that," Snude replied. "A fire up here could be seen for miles."

"What's the difference?" Quintada growled. "We're not going to get into the Superstitions without being seen."

"Probably not," Snude conceded, "but the less attention we attract the better."

We had fetched along a tent to give Serafina some privacy but, when Snude offered to have someone put it up, the girl shook her head. "This wouldn't be the first time I've slept on the ground or" — she added — "gone without supper."

For breakfast we chewed some more jerky. With the mules repacked and the stars still blinking as energetically as ever, we got underway a good two hours short of dawn.

Spartokori edged his horse nearer mine. "What's the hell-tearin' rush?"

I had no idea and said so.

"These animals ought to have more rest. My backbone's rubbin' a hole in my belly," he grumbled. "If this keeps up, we're going to have to do something!"

"What've you got in mind?"

He gave me a scowl in the brightening light and wheeled his

19

gelding to take off after Cookson who was first in line behind Quintada and the tails of the mules.

We were climbing steadily into higher country, though barely discernible until one looked behind at the pitch. There was a lot of rock here with spruce and scraggly pines growing out of it, and the sky seemed bluer than it had down below.

I got to thinking about Jacob Walzer, the Dutchman, who had died in 1891 — old Jake and his burros tramping their lonely way through the legends that had grown up about him. Still an enigma, he was a man whose character would seem to have changed as often as the stories in which he'd played a part. Lining up around here for some time, I'd heard most of them and still couldn't separate fact from baloney; everything about him had been exaggerated. The only thing you knew for sure were the burro loads of gold he'd brought out of the Superstitions.

Thousands had searched for the source of that ore and come out even poorer than when they'd gone in. Rock piled on rock, these were as grim a batch of mountains as I'd ever been into, steeped in the hush of centuries, their silence seldom broken by anything louder than the scream of an eagle's prey or the hair-raising yammer of some distant coyote. A vast desolation of sun-bleached rock and twisted cañons where more than a few had lost their lives.

It was sometime in the 1870s when the tales about Jake and his fabulous mine began to spread like ripples from a stone plummeting into still water. No one remembers who started them now; they grew like the wonderful beans Jack planted, a habit of rumors and oft-told tales.

Facts were few and hard to come by. In 1864 Walzer had been living in Prescott. Based on records — and the truth of this attested by our hot-to-trot banker — Walzer between 1880 and 1889 had shipped more than 250,000 dollars' worth of gold ore to the mint and was buried now in a Phoenix cemetery.

Aware that Jake had been on the territory's tax rolls for over twenty-five years, I figured more facts should be available, but these were all I'd been able to come up with. Of those who had known him, and there'd been quite a few, they mostly pictured him with beard and steel-rimmed glasses and to be a murdering scoundrel straight out of hell. Others described him as highly intelligent, well educated, a compassionate man. But from all reports he was not a good mixer, kept to himself, and had so few close friends I'd not been able to put a name even to one of them.

At about this point in my cogitations the girl dropped back on her gray horse to say Snude would like to have a few words with me, so I followed her up to where he rode at the head of the line. He gave me a nod and spoke in his brusque fashion.

"Those buildings off to the right a couple miles are the Circle Dot headquarters. The new owner, man named Flake, came to the bank last week for a loan . . . wants a Hereford bull to breed up his herd. Had to turn him down, but I'm inclined right now to think I might oblige him. It's in my mind to drop over there and have a look at the place." He saw I didn't think much of this notion. "All I'm asking you to do is find a good place for us to camp up ahead, get the mules unloaded, and have somebody get a supper fire started. A small one," he said. "Be dark pretty soon."

"Any reason you can't see this feller on the way back?"

"He might make other arrangements by then. Don't know how long we'll have to spend in those mountains."

I didn't like any part of this. I couldn't help wondering what he was up to and knew the others wouldn't like it any better than I did.

"Going to cause a lot of talk," I told him bluntly. "Wouldn't do it, if I were you."

He rummaged my face with an irritable stare. "Why not?"

21

"Just told you. Bound to cause talk. Looks fishy as hell after all the duckin' and dodgin' we've done."

You could see plain enough he was considerably put out. After chewing his lip a couple of moments, he jerked me a nod and kicked his horse into motion.

When I got back to the others, Spartokori kneed his mount alongside mine, wanted to know why I'd been sent for. As I've likely mentioned, most of them knew I'd poked around through the gulches and cañons below Fish Creek, so I passed it off as a need for directions.

"Guess he's not too familiar with the country hereabouts. Wanted to know how to reach the old Peralta Road."

"Man would think he'd want you at the front."

I chucked him a grin. "Serafina's better lookin'."

"Well, you're right about that. Just the same. . . ?"

Behind us Cookson said, "I'd give a handful of pennies to know what that so-and-so's got up his sleeve."

"Expect it's his arm."

"Yeah. Very funny." He rasped a hand across his chin. "You honestly think he expects to find that mine?"

"Honestly, no. I believe what he hopes to get hold of through that map the girl's got is one of those old Peralta mines."

Spartokori snorted, and Cookson said, "That's damn' near as crazy. With all the hungry lookers that's hunted Walzer's mine in the last fifty years, if ever there was any Peralta mines, one of them anyway should have been discovered."

"Not necessarily. You're forgetting the Apaches. No one's the equal of a redskin at hiding things. They didn't want palefaces prowlin' those mountains, which is why they polished off the Peraltas' outfit. Only one to escape was the girl's uncle, Gonzales, who as luck would have it wasn't with the rest of them."

Cookson looked pretty skeptical.

I said, "I'm convinced the Peraltas had mines around there

some place. They knew that last time when they brought in that bunch of peons to speed up the diggin' those Apaches were getting restless. It's my suspicion each night, when they quit work, they took the ore they'd recovered and hid it some place they figured wouldn't be found. The Dutchman's gold, way I see it, come out of that cache. If we can believe a quarter of the stories, old Jake was an educated man, a mining engineer with a deal of practical experience."

"You believe that?"

"Sure I believe it. In different parts of Europe, where mines have been worked, his name is on the records. Might have been pure luck that caused him to stumble onto it, but I'm convinced he knew what to look for."

Spartokori said, scowling, "If you're right about that, we might as well go home."

I told him straight-faced, "No one's standin' on your shirttail. I've got two hundred bucks invested in this venture and, if anything's found, I aim to collect my share. Snude and the girl seem convinced the Dutchman's gold came from one of the Peralta mines. I figure it come from one of those hiding places. That map of Serafina's ought to put us pretty close."

"If those quakes," Cookson said, "didn't shake up all the landmarks."

Considering the general drift of their remarks, there was another little "if" that had to do with the alleged Peralta map. I didn't bother going into it.

We camped that night beside a stretch of Queen Creek some three hours southwest of where the Peralta Road would be crossed some years later by Federal Highway 60. There was plenty of brush and, despite Snude's objections, we built up a small fire of dry sticks and had ourselves the first real meal since leaving the O. K. Corral.

With the mules unloaded, I helped Quintada put up the girl's tent and was rewarded by a smile that pushed the blood through my veins like a shot of Old Crow. Fully aware it was given without thought and held no special meaning, I was still young enough to start counting chickens that would probably never hatch.

Not long after eating she took a little walk. When she returned, she went into the tent and dropped the flap. The rest of the outfit rolled up in their soogans, myself included. For a while, hunting sleep, that smile was warmly in my head. Then, with a darkening mood in my mind, I looked again at Ebbert Snude. The next I knew Snude's hectoring voice was ordering all of us up to get the packs on the mules and be on our way.

Leaving the creek, we were back in the desert, picking our way for an hour through stands of greasewood, cholla, and the gray leafless wands of wolf's candle until even these disappeared. There was nothing to see in our immediate vicinity but clumps of pear and low shaggy tops of mesquites, half buried where forgotten winds had left them clothed in mounds of sand.

With a breeze springing up and the sun knee high above the southern scarp of Iron Mountain off to our right, even these were left behind and nothing was directly ahead of us except sand and, sticking up out of it, a distant blue, the sharp skinny top of Weaver's Needle.

When we reached the Peralta Road, which was no more than a path left by burros and easily missed, I loped up to where Snude rode with Serafina and pointed it out. Beneath a brassy sky with the sun midway to noon, we followed this trace toward Weaver's Needle with Superstition Mountain off to the left and its satellite hills, buttes, peaks, and mountains rearing up through a haze almost everywhere you looked.

We were still in the desert. From where we'd turned off on this burro path, there were seven long miles between us and the Needle, and these were not the sort to be traversed in haste.

24

It was close to noon, still some two miles short of it, when the narrow cañon named for the Peraltas opened off to the left, running along the east flank of the double-peaked length of Superstition Mountain. Here we stopped for a breather.

"You got any idea where we're at?" Snude asked.

"Near as I can figure," I told him, "we're about where the Peraltas must have made their main camp — their first one, I mean, from where they set out to search for the gold they found."

"You aim to go into that rock-ribbed gut?" Schroeder wanted to know.

Snude, looking dubious, turned to the girl. "Let's see that map." When she handed it to him and he'd got it smoothed out, he said after studying it a moment, "That's the way to Weaver's Needle, through this cañon, and Weaver's Needle appears to be the tall sharp peak referred to. Their nearest mine seems to be north of it — no measurement here to say how far."

Spartokori and Schroeder crowded up to peer over his shoulder.

"What good's a map," Spartokori growled, "that don't show how far one thing is from the next?"

"Might not even be Weaver's Needle," Schroeder grumbled and looked at me.

I said, "It's no longer known when that name was tacked onto it. Captain Weaver, a French trapper and scout, was first heard of in what is now Arizona sometime early in the 1830s. It's not known when he was in the Superstitions. Don Miguel's three sons are said to have started placer operations in or along the Salt River above these mountains early in the 1840s. I doubt if at that time this peak had any name other than whatever the Apaches called it. Miner's Needle or Tortilla Mountain could just as well have been the tall sharp peak described."

"It's even taller than Weaver's, according to a topographical map I have dated 1900," Cookson remarked. "But whatever peak the Peraltas had in mind, it don't butter no parsnips far as we're concerned. To say this mine's to the north of it is about as much use as a twenty-two cartridge in a twelve gauge shotgun."

Serafina mentioned that some of the mines did have dimensions from prominent landmarks, but there again unless those landmarks were still visible those too were useless. Since we were right at the mouth of it, they elected to push on through this cañon to where it became East Boulder Cañon and start our hunt north of Weaver's Needle which, as I recalled, would be somewhere around Black Top Mountain.

There was a lot of brush interspersed with saguaros and palo verdes around the entrance to this cañon and, even after we got into it, we found the going pretty rugged and had to pick our way through a deal of fallen rock, in some places almost preventing further progress. In fact, once into this passage about all you could see was rock, a lot of it standing on end and some places so choked it was difficult to see how we could get through it. Getting the horses past jumbles of tumbled rock was even more of a tribulation. We had to get off and lead each one snorting, blowing, and rolling his eyes. Had anyone coughed, I believe they'd have bolted. Working through that cañon was a nerve-racking business, and yet it was the route supposedly taken by those Spanish Peraltas in getting their gold back home to Sonora.

Schroeder called to the banker, "Better find some other way of getting us out of here. Be god-damned easy to find ourselves afoot!"

Snude only grunted: "If you're afraid of this country, don't come into it."

Schroeder, with a long hard look, managed to keep his mouth shut, which I thought was a blessing with tempers already stretched tight as fiddle strings.

It was mighty near dark when we finally got into the wide

open stretch that separates the Needle from Black Top Mountain. The last half hour of that nightmare journey had been over the relatively boulder-free floor of East Boulder Cañon, and to the east across this desolate stretch of sand and burro weed was the parallel cut of Needle Cañon, according to the best of my recollection.

"We'll be camping right here for a spell," Snude decided. "Let's get those mules unloaded, Pepe. I'll put up the tent while the rest of you scout up some stuff to make a fire with. What we need's a good meal under our belts."

That last was cheering news to all hands. I helped Quintana get the packs off the mules and, afterwards, helped him water the animals from out of our hats. Snude had chosen a dry camp to squat.

Cookson, whom the banker had volunteered to be cook, produced in due course a big pot of boiled beans, two pans of biscuits about as fluffy as hardtack, and a pair of skinny jackrabbits Schroeder had dropped for him. This bountiful repast was eaten for the most part in shuddery silence, after which we rolled into our blankets and slept.

Chapter Four

"A MAN NAMED FLAKE"

The sun was up when Snude, having overslept, roused us out of our blankets. Someone built up a fire and for breakfast Bob served up refried beans and what was left of those petrified biscuits, during which the banker informed us we were now north of Weaver's Needle. Pepe was to remain in camp with Serafina to keep an eye on our livestock. The rest of us would begin our hunt for the Number One Mine. I had to smile to myself. He was going to find out there was a deal more to prospecting than had ever occurred to him sitting behind his big desk at the bank.

We spent the whole day poking around through the brush and rocks. No crevice or hollow was overlooked, and not even the smell of a mine did we uncover. It was discouraging work made even more aggravating with that sun glaring down and the random breeze trickling through those rocks nearly as hot as a stove lid.

The only encouraging note came after we had quit and, stinking with sweat, arrived back at camp to discover Serafina had cooked up a supper of rabbit stew liberally sprinkled with diced potatoes, tinned tomatoes, and a bit of wild mustard she had managed to find. The meal was topped off with tinned peaches and biscuits that practically melted in our mouths.

Cookson declared with a teasing grin, "I'd never have guessed you were such a good cook, Pepe."

Quintada said, "All I done was catch the rabbits. Knocked

three of them over with a single shot."

With that elegant repast inside us, we were able to laugh for the first time that day — even Spartokori who wasn't much given to laughter at any time.

Schroeder said, "I vote we make Miz Peralta our official cook."

"Tomorrow," Snude said, "we'll range farther afield," and looked around at me. "Reckon we ought to tackle that next cañon?"

Shrugging, I said: "Needle Cañon, you mean? Wouldn't do any harm. Flanks Bluff Spring Mountain along its east side. It'll be considerably wider than what we've been through. With all the folks that have been hunting this country, I doubt we'll find anything that's not been prowled over. Most of my own trips didn't fetch me west of Music Mountain, the next one east of Bluff Spring, about a half mile north of Herman. If we move north, beyond what we covered today, we'll be approaching the Red Hills or, turning east, there's Black Mountain."

Serafina produced her map. The second mine discovered by the Peralta brothers looked to be on a southern slope marked Red Hills.

"Might as well try for that," Schroeder muttered.

"First," Snude said, "we'll prospect the north side of that next mountain east of us and the south flank of what this map calls Black Mountain."

"In that case," I said, "we better camp at the spring. If we can find it. . . ."

Spartokori, nodding, said, "Another dry camp and we'll be running short of water, the way these animals been lappin' it up."

So the next morning, with our supplies, tools, tent, and bedding packed on the mules, we set off to find the spring on Bluff Spring Mountain. We got an early start to avoid having to travel during the worst of the heat which down in these cañons we'd found to be pretty fierce.

For the first three hours we were relatively comfortable. Then the morning breeze whipping down off the higher altitudes withered away and, by the time we'd left Needle Cañon and started around the mountain's northern flank with the Red Hills distantly shimmering to our left, the heat was building up fast.

Before we had gone more than another half mile, we came to the scree-covered slope of an ancient slide and, by climbing this, were able to get ourselves and our animals onto a sort of terrace that led off in an easterly direction through lodgepole pines. In the next quarter hour this opened up into a kind of glen filled with knee-high grass and a large pool of sparkling water fed by a spring trickling from a crevice in the rocks higher up.

"I guess we're on the bluff," Cookson said, looking around.

Snude decided, "We'll camp right here. Get the packs off the mules. Watch out they don't founder themselves on that water. . . ."

Quintada cut in to say, "A horse might do that, but mules has better sense."

Snude ignored this. As head of the oldest financial firm in the area, he'd grown accustomed to ignoring things he didn't want to hear. He said, "I'll be going back down for a preliminary look. I'll take Spartokori and Schroeder along while the rest of you get the camp set up and keep your eyes peeled."

Once the three had gone off on their horses and Cookson was busy putting up the girl's tent while engaging her in chitchat, Quintada and myself — apparently the peons of this outfit — occupied ourselves with watering the stock.

Pepe said under his breath, "Listening to him, you'd think some bogie with a gun was back of every bush! You got any idea who owns that spread you and him was starin' at a couple days ago?"

30

"Said it had a new owner, fellow named Flake, anxious for a loan to buy a registered bull. Snude was proposin' to go down and have a look at the place till I talked him out of it."

"Good thing you did," Pepe said darkly. "Ben Flake's the whelp of that Silverlock ranny that with Goldlock recovered fifteen thousand dollars' worth of ore from the Massacre Grounds way the hell back. Flake's mama was Apache and the less he knows about us the better."

"Bad lot, is he?"

"Ain't my place to blacken anybody's character, but he's one son of a bitch we don't want any truck with. And while we're on the subject, keep a bag of salt handy whenever that banker starts warmin' up to you. Bugger would pick your teeth for what gold you got in 'em!"

Peering up at the crest above the sixty-degree climb through shattered rock a man would have to make to get up there made it hardly appear to be worth the effort. Great blocks of weather-broken stone cracked by countless centuries of erosion lay all over the face of this shale-littered slope. Staring at that depressing view, I almost turned back — it appeared so unlikely.

A great place for snakes. It wasn't even the right kind of rock, a metamorphose argillite thrust in eons past from some prehistoric sea, an opaque quartz extremely unlikely to conceal what had brought us here, even more unlikely to have caught the attention of the hordes who had hunted the Dutchman's mine. Yet an old saying held that gold was where you found it. With no prospect of discovering anything of value, some random notion I could not pin down urged me to tackle that precarious maze.

Fully aware that a careless step could break a leg or find me the victim of some frightened rattler, I worked my perspiring way toward the peak without uncovering the least thing of interest. With a whole hour wasted and a good twenty yards still short of the top, I stopped once more to catch my breath.

Panting, disgusted, I gave it up, bitterly regretting the wasted energy. Hoping to find a better way down, I moved off to the right toward the western flank, doubly cautious now, being watched by a buzzard coasting by on spread wings as it circled the crown.

I quartered the slope with sweat-blurred stare, sleeved my dripping face, and stared again. The pitch at this point appeared slightly less hazardous. With the spread-winged shadow sailing past me again, I stopped in my tracks, my glance caught by the sight of a near-black hole some yards ahead and three strides lower down, some sort of opening, too large for a coyote, too small for a bear.

Only mildly excited, I considered it for some further moments before gingerly picking my way a bit nearer. Nothing recent about it, the weathered edges of this opening had been exposed a long while.

Curiosity pulled me nearer, dropped me into a crouch. From this close-up squat with the sun behind me, it appeared to be the opening to some sort of cave. Gripped by the thought of Jake Walzer's gold, I threw caution to the winds and crawled inside.

It was a cave, all right, but one enlarged by man. Upright again, in the light of a cupped match, I could see where rock had been hacked off the walls, but the slanting floor held no debris. Striking a second match, I found its width to be roughly ten feet and the depth of it nearer twenty with no opening but the one I'd come in by. Whatever the reason this space had been enlarged, it must, I reckoned, have been the work of someone with adequate tools. There were no signs of fire and stone implements could hardly have made a dent in the rock that had been removed. Striking another match, I scrutinized the floor. Nothing had disturbed this dust in years.

Peraltas, or their peons, may have gouged these walls and,

finding nothing of interest, abandoned the place. About to do likewise in considerable of a letdown, I stubbed one foot on a hump in the floor, lost my balance, and crashed into a wall.

Shaking my head, I leaned there a moment waiting for the dizziness to pass. Recovering, pushing myself away from the wall, I felt something give. Not much, but enough to catch at my attention. Turning around, astonished, I stared at the wall with the aid of a fresh match. I ran a finger along what appeared to be a seam, broken in several places by the force of my impact.

It was, indeed, exactly what it looked to be, a seam plastered over with a mixture of clay and crushed limestone that until I'd rammed into it had certainly not been noticeable. With my hunting knife, fairly tingling with anticipation, I scraped away the plaster to find myself eyeing an oblong slab of rock someone had painstakingly set into the wall to conceal whatever lay behind it. The slab was approximately four feet by two.

There was no guessing how thick it might be. Obviously it was a close fit, since none of my thumpings managed to budge it. Having used the last of my matches, I stood in the dim light of this place with my mind in an uproar, still staring at my discovery for perhaps a dozen minutes, considering the implications.

For the amount of work someone had gone to something pretty valuable almost certainly was behind it. Though it hardly made sense, the Dutchman's mine was the first thing I thought of. Not all of my pushing moved that stone another fraction. Without some kind of bar or sledge, there was just no way I could learn what I'd stumbled onto.

My next clear thought had to do with sharing, and I have to admit this was not a thought that pleased me. I wanted to keep the whole thing to myself, to return at some later time and pack off whatever was back of that slab. But with that plaster dug away, what if someone else happened onto it?

Chapter Five

THE CLANDESTINE PARTNER

All the way down I kept going over it. Finders keepers — the creed of the treasure hunter from time immemorial. Why should I share it with the others in this outfit? Any one of them, had he stumbled on such a find, would have kept his damn' mouth shut. The only real drawback to keeping my own shut was the unlikely possibility of someone else's blundering onto it.

Back at our camp beside the pool it was plain that the trio who'd been scouting the cañon had found nothing worth discussion. They were all sitting around with glum faces waiting for Serafina to dish up the grub.

Looking them over, I said as I found myself a seat, "How'd it go? You discover anything?"

Spartokori, scowling, growled, "About as much as I'd expect to find in those trashy rocks you've been hunting."

Snude, looking up from the girl's faded map, said, "If you'd taken a halfway look at this thing, you'd have known going up there was just wasting your time."

In an offhand fashion I said, "A man never knows where lightning will strike," — and got onto my feet.

Cookson laughed, and across the fire I could see Serafina, gone completely still, considering me with a peculiar look.

Spartokori snorted. "You damn' well never found nothing up there!"

"Oh, but I did."

Now I had their fullest attention. With that beard and all,

you could seldom tell what Cookson was thinking, but incredulity had dropped Snude's jaw and the Greek got up with a disbelieving sneer. "An Indian arrowhead?"

"A mite better than that. Would you settle for a cave?"

"Not the right formation for a cave up there," Snude said, dismissing it.

But Cookson's glance was still searching my face. "What sort of cave?"

"A little bigger than nature made it."

Of a sudden I had too much attention. Snude said, irascibly, "You been at those cactus buds?"

I was wishing I'd kept my find to myself and was about to pass it off with a grin when Cookson, scanning that rock-strewn slope, quietly asked, "How big is this cave, Chuck? Anything in it?"

"About ten by twenty. I lit a few matches. Dust on the floor. Didn't see any tracks." This, I figured, ought to wash out their interest.

But Cookson said, with a cute little grin more than half hidden behind those black whiskers, "I've boned up on this subject. There are a number of caves in the Superstitions, but nobody's mentioned one on Bluff Spring Mountain. You sure it's a cave?"

I shrugged. "Looked like it might have been a cave originally. I expect it's been widened, probably a long while ago."

Snude said, "Then it's been gone over from top to bottom whether you saw tracks or not." Frowning, he added, "How high up?"

"Pretty near to the top."

He shook his head.

Spartokori remarked in a thoughtful tone, "Didn't find any artifacts up there, did you? Pots, stone tools, anything like that?"

"Wasn't nothing up there but dust that I could see."

"Still, a cave's a cave," Cookson murmured as though thinking aloud, "and, in this set of circumstances, hardly to be dismissed without another look. If you'll take me up there first thing in the morning, I'll be glad to help you go over it again. Never know . . . might come onto something you missed."

"Fat chance," Spartokori jeered with a resentful look in my direction. "This ain't the first prospect Brannigan's been on. If there was anything there, he'd have seen it."

I managed another shrug.

"Grub's ready, boys," Serafina called.

We all got up and trooped over to the fire. Cookson's proposal had put the hawk among the pigeons and no mistake. I must have left tracks all over the place. He stood by with his pan while I was filling mine then, adroitly steering me off among the trees, said: "This'll do," and sat down beside me. "Reckon we'll need a light up there?"

"Surprised you'd want to make such a climb just to look at an empty cave, Bob."

"Call it a hunch," he grinned. "We going to need a light?"

"If you expect to see anything, you certain sure will and, if you figure to do any digging up there, you better fetch along a pick or a bar."

He quit chewing to give me a look. "You mean like a crow-bar?"

"That's what I had in mind. Not much point in going up there empty handed."

He went on with his eating. Then he said, "There is something up there." He stared at me a while. With another of those half hidden grins he remarked, "Though you didn't see anything of value, you suspect . . . ?"

"Look," I said, "if you're bound to go up there, I may as well tell you I uncovered a door someone had plastered over. They made such a good job of it I can't help feelin' they'd not have gone to such bother without they'd left something back

36

of it they didn't want found."

"No one can argue with that sort of logic. Just what do you expect is back of it? Surely not the residue of Montezuma's treasure the Indians hid from those Spanish bandits supposedly here to civilize them? The Hohokams, then?"

"I don't reckon we need go back that far. You've certainly heard stories of gold being hidden by Apaches. I was thinking it possible some of that. . . ."

Nodding, Cookson broke in, "Quite possible. You may even have hit on what's back of it . . . might even be the source of Walzer's gold, though I'm inclined to doubt that."

"To get at it we'll at least need a bar of some sort, something heavy enough to get out that slab. But unless we deal the others in, they'll be suspicious as hell if we go up there with any kind of a tool."

This fetched me another of his sly little grins. "Leave it to me," he said with a wink, and went back toward the fire with his empty pan.

If only I'd kept my damn' mouth shut! Perhaps, too, it was just as well that I hadn't. Without help — even with a bar — one man alone would probably not be able to remove that slab or set it back in again after examining what was back of it. If there was gold hidden back of it, it was going to have to stay where it was a while longer. There was no easy way we could remove any worthwhile amount without being detected.

If I had to have a clandestine partner, Bob Cookson was plainly the best of the lot. Shrewd, tough minded, quick to catch on, with his wits and my experience we should have no trouble in bringing this off. He was, I guessed, about my own age, but unmistakably smarter, a man with a bunch of irons in the fire, most of which he managed to keep out of sight. Pretty well off by all indications, he dealt in old and rare books in a second-hand store in the heart of the Old Pueblo. Sophisticated and

37

knowledgeable, the greatest drawback to Bob as a partner was the question of how far I'd be able to trust him in the event we found anything worth real money. And that was the rub.

It was too late to back out of going up there with him. It was already too late soon as, goaded by the jeers of Spartokori and Snude, I'd mentioned the cave. If I refused now to go up there again, it would only start talk and speculation among the others which might end up with the whole bunch going up. Cookson was going to have a look at it anyway — even if I'd said nothing about the door I'd uncovered.

It took me that night a long while to get to sleep and, when I'd finally drifted off, it seemed I'd hardly shut my eyes when a rough hand kept at me till I opened them again to find Cookson's black-whiskered face bending over me.

"Quiet, or you'll have the whole camp up. Took some doing, but I've got a bar for each of us."

Throwing off my cover, I'd scarcely got to my feet when he thrust a crowbar into my hand.

"Lead away. I'll be right behind you."

That gave me several more notions to add to my collection. Moving in the deeper shadows of the pines and keeping down wind of our hobbled transport, we crept nervously along the bluff until the mountain's shoulder hid us from our snoring companions.

"You bring a torch?"

"Fetched two," he said in what was practically a whisper, and handed me one which I promptly pocketed.

By this time that crowbar's weight seemed to have increased considerably. "Where's yours?" I asked, discovering now, as we moved out of the trees toward the place where I'd come down off the mountain, that neither of his hands held anything.

"Got it hooked to my belt. Couldn't find but one full-size one. Mine's a jimmy . . . kind of figured it might come in handy.

Think that moon will give enough light to climb by?"

"We can't use torches on this open slope."

"Guess not," he muttered, peering up at the acres of broken rock above us. "Hell of a mess. I'll give odds no one else ever tackled this mountain."

I said over my shoulder, "Anybody takes you up on that, you might as well put yourself in the poorhouse. There's been more than one up there, that's for certain. Somebody dug through that wall. Better watch your footin'."

"Better watch out for snakes. I hear they're night crawlers."

"Only snakes on my mind are the ones we left in camp. You know what'll happen if we're caught doing this."

"Like to be a first rate row," Cookson chuckled. "We might even get to see a few corpses. How you fixed for cartridges?"

I was in no mood for that brand of joke. It cut entirely too close to the real possibilities. "This bunch's not the sort to stamp your boot at."

Conversation after that kind of withered on the vine. What with panting and sweating, trying to relocate the cave, and keep from breaking a leg in this treacherous moon glow — plus one of them back there possibly waking up and spotting us — I'd no mind left for idle chitchat.

Getting up that mountain had been difficult enough the first time I'd tackled it. Hiking through this maze of shattered rock at night seemed to take forever. Everything looked different, and I began to wonder if, weighted down with that damned bar, I'd be able to find it. As it happened, I overshot the place. Back and forth I went like a chicken with its head off. It was only when I looked over my shoulder to see where Bob was that I spotted it and put out a pointing hand.

"Christ," he panted, peering toward what in this light seemed scarcely bigger than a rabbit hole, "I'd begun to think you were giving me the run around! Mean to say that's the entrance?"

39

Chucking the crowbar into it and dropping to all fours, I wriggled in after it, hearing his grunts as he followed my example and got to his feet in the light of my torch.

"Damn!" he said, staring at the slab my knife had uncovered. "Aren't they likely to see this light?"

"Don't think so. Camp's not in sight from up here."

Moving closer, he inspected the slab. "Pretty neat job they made of it," he mumbled. "Expect you're right about the age of this work. Walzer never done it. Hohokam probably. Could have been Spaniards . . . the Peraltas I'd guess, if they had enough patience." Showing his first excitement, "Let's get at it," he said, unslinging the jimmy he'd had hooked to his belt. "Pretty chilly up here. Going to take some doing to get that chunk out. Wonder how the hell they lifted it in there."

He tapped it lightly with his jimmy. "Damnation!" he growled, trying to slip the prizing end of the bar into the bottom seam and obviously unable to do it. "Don't know if we can get this bugger out or not."

"Here, let me have a whack at it."

Handing him my torch and taking a good grip on the bar, I looked again at a chipped place along the vertical right-hand seam where pressure, apparently, had snapped a tiny fragment from the face of the slab. I tried to slip the curved end of the bar into the seam at this point. I couldn't get any purchase. Reversing the jimmy, I had better luck, managing to insert the sharp end into the slit perhaps a quarter of an inch.

I said, "Put down your light and get hold of that crowbar. That's right. Tap the curved end of this bar . . . not too hard now. Just enough to. . . . That's it, that ought to be plenty."

He stood back. By applying steady pressure, I moved that whole side of the slab outward, toward us, by about half an inch.

"Try the other side," I said, taking the crowbar and handing him the jimmy.

It seemed for awhile that this left-hand side would resist all our efforts. But in the end, between us, we finally managed to fetch it out a noisy inch. In the quiet of the night that grating racket seemed much louder than it was. With extreme care I prized my side of the slab, aiming to bring it out an equal distance. Perhaps the stone wasn't fitted quite as snugly along this side. It moved more easily than I'd expected. I had to drop the jimmy and grab at the stone. It did not, luckily, come all the way out and get away from me — the reason I'd been in such a sweat to lay hold of it. My side was the only part that came out, about four inches from the wall it had been set into. But now that we could get hold of the rascal, we managed to lift it out without losing a limb in the process.

Leaning it out of our way against the wall, we shone the light of both torches into the considerable space it had covered. For a long moment, incapable of speech, we stood locked in our tracks, staring at things concealed by dead hands for longer perhaps than both our ages combined.

Naked greed isn't something a man often thinks about and never, probably, in connection with himself, yet I believe, peering into that cache, both of us felt a nearly ungovernable desire. On an outburst of breath Bob was the first to break whatever it was that had hold of us. We couldn't know yet if what we'd uncovered was worth the effort nor did we guess, I'm sure, what this discovery could do.

We saw four bulging sailcloth sacks, one back of the other, ranged along one whole side of the cavity. The remaining space was occupied by a number of baked clay jars of various dimensions, obviously old and almost certainly produced by Indians; gray these were with black symbols or patterns, the largest pair about two feet tall by ten or twelve inches across.

Tugging the nearest one toward him, Cookson shone his light into it and sound broke out of him, unconscionably loud in the

41

eerie quiet of that place. The jar appeared filled to within an inch of the top with tarnished coins, Spanish *reales* — pieces of eight.

We were both, I guess, pretty tense with excitement. I damn' sure was. I found it difficult to breathe. There is something about the sight of hidden treasure that unexplainably takes hold of a person, often altering his outlook. Like whiskey, bringing up buried instincts, changing sometimes a whole personality. I don't say that's how it was with us but, looking back, I think in that moment it sowed the seeds of a mutual distrust.

The other largest jar was farther back, surrounded by smaller ones. The biggest of the smaller ones was about six inches high and possibly five inches wide at the open mouth, crammed with crudely cut stones of spiderweb turquoise. The rest of the jars, set cheek by jowl in what space was left, were about four by four, all but the smallest one of the lot which I picked up myself and found half filled with emerald cabochons, mostly flawed as we discovered when I poured out a handful. The four by fours, of which there were twelve, were filled with coins, Spanish doubloons minted in Mexico, *pistoles,* and sterling *reales.*

The doubloons were worth ten dollars U. S. "Probably more," Cookson said, "as Spartokori would say, to collectors." These were gold, like the *pistoles.* "Not a bad haul. Let's have a look at what's in the sacks."

"Don't you reckon we better start back?"

"I suppose," he mumbled, "but let's take a look." He reached for the nearest, but the canvas was rotten and split when he tugged. "Christ!" he exclaimed.

I said, "Damn!" — staring at what had spilled from the sack. "If that's not gold ore, I'll eat it!"

Back of those whiskers it wasn't easy to make out his expression, but I needed no crystal ball to guess he was far from delighted. There'd been no reason to imagine I'd stumbled onto Jake

Walzer's mine, but dollars to doughnuts the possibility was what had fetched him up here.

"Buck up," I said. "We're not doing too bad. Whatever it amounts to, we're a heap better off than those buggers down below. This could cut up pretty rich."

He threw me a sour look. "It's a long way short of the risk we've run if Snude or Spartokori find out what we been up to!"

I stared at him, astonished. "If that's goin' to put your bowels in an uproar, there's nothing to stop us cuttin' them in. You came up here thinking I might have missed something and found you were right when you discovered the slab hidden back of that plaster. They'll swallow that, I reckon."

"Well . . . the hell with them!" he growled. "We're not obligated to share this with them!"

"Better make up your mind. Time's a-wastin'. If we're not cutting them in, we better get back there before we're missed."

"What are we going to do about this?" he grumbled, waving a hand at the hole we had opened.

"Have to put that slab back." I shut off my torch and thrust it into my belt. "Set your light on the floor and give me a hand."

The stone was not half as thick as I'd imagined. Grunting, we soon had it back in place.

"We better leave that crowbar in case someone's awake," I remarked.

He still wasn't satisfied, scowling at the obvious signs of our handiwork. "If one of them comes up here. . . ."

"Hell's fire!" I said.

"All right . . . all right. Let's get out of here."

Chapter Six

SADDLE TRAMPS

The flimsy grays of false dawn were already visible off to the east by the time we got down into the pines, and Quintada was already building up the fire when I retrieved my soogans and sauntered into camp. I chucked him a nod.

"For treasure hunters," I said, "this bunch sure's not much for early rising."

Above his bandit's mustache I thought our mule man's stare looked downright suspicious. "Where you sleep las' night, *hombre?*"

I dredged up a chuckle. "Down the trail a piece . . . why? Looking for me?"

"You see Cookson?"

"Yeah. Like the rest of this outfit . . . still pounding his ear." I waved a hand toward the cottonwoods beyond the pool. "I never seen such a bunch."

"What you want to sleep down there for?"

"Somebody ought to keep an eye peeled." He turned away with a grunt, and I dropped my bedroll beside the mound of supplies we'd unpacked. "You know if Snude figures to be here again today?"

He threw some more wood on the fire. "Told me he thought he'd check out your cave," he said, giving me a look from the corners of his eyes.

"Snude ask you to keep an eye up on me?"

His eyes turned shifty.

I said, "You better walk soft if you want to keep eating. I carry a big stick."

Hard to say if he swallowed that. Snude, still buttoning his shirt, was striding in our direction, and just then Serafina came out of the tent. Quintada, as though he'd just remembered something, clapped a hand to his forehead and went hustling off.

"Mornin', boss."

Looking irritably after the departing wrangler, the banker grunted. "What was that all about?"

"Couldn't make head nor tails of his jabber. Seemed like he was saying you was figurin' to have a look at that cave. Want to go up now?"

"No, I don't. And I'm not waiting around for you to take Cookson, either. Soon as we've eaten and filled up our water bags, we're heading for Black Mountain."

Schroeder, some place behind me, said, "Be a heap smarter to have us a look at them Red Hills. Nothin' on that mountain but lava, basalt, an' volcanic ash."

When Snude's head swung irascibly toward him, Schroeder growled, "Check with your mule boy if you won't take my word for it. Claims he's been all over that pile."

Serafina, coming up to us then, said, "Don Miguel's map doesn't show anything there, nor in the Red Hills. But Uncle Gonzales once told me he'd found color in those hills while prospecting there."

Snude dug out the map and pored over it a spell and, while he was studying it, Quintada came up with a scowl to ask, "When we eat, eh?"

Schroeder drawled, "Now that's a good question. Where's Cookson got to?"

"Right here," Bob said. "Reckon I overslept. I'll get right at it. . . ."

The banker, folding up the map, declared, "No time for that

now. We'll have a good meal after we're located. Get the mules packed, Pepe. We'll take a look in those Red Hills Schroeder mentioned."

Shortly after noon we got a close-up look at those damned hills and, peering at their sugarloaf shapes with the red earth showing between the grass clumps, I figured prowling the dirt streets of Tucson would turn up as much as we were likely to find here. It was hard to be at my cheerful best with a headful of notions that wouldn't let go of me, chief and foremost of which was the nasty conviction the cave I had stupidly shot off my mouth about wasn't likely to remain unvisited until we could manage to get back to it. What we had found might be no great fortune, but my half would have easily kept me in comfort for the next several years, and the chance of someone else getting their hands on it was a constant distraction.

Another thing bothering me was Snude's impatience. I could see no reason for this unless he figured he had an inside track to the source of Walzer's fabulous ore. It seemed plain he felt about these Red Hills the same contempt he had shown for that mountain, so why was he wasting our time riding into them? Why not make straight for old Jake's bonanza?

He'd said the girl was with us because of her map, but the map did not show any mine in these hills. I could see he set great store by that map, but to me even if it was authentic — had actually been drawn by Miguel Peralta — too much time had gone by for it to have any value since it must have been drawn before those quakes.

Another thing bothering me was the searching looks directed at me by that black-browed Quintada. I'd no idea what had aroused his suspicions, but it was a cinch something had, and I meant to make sure he'd latch onto no opportunity to get back to that cave ahead of me. I was getting just as impatient as Snude looked to be.

When it came right down to it, a bird in the hand appeared a heap better to me than any number of birds tucked away in the bushes. I couldn't believe we had the ghost of a chance of discovering the source of the Dutchman's gold. So why had I let Snude talk me into this?

With Snude in the lead and Serafina directly behind him and Schroeder as it happened right on the heels of the horse she was riding, we went into the gap between the first pair of hills. There was plenty of room going through this ravine to ride two abreast like a cavalry column, but we went in single file, the mules with their packs strung out behind Schroeder. Next after the mules was that mustached Quintada, then myself, with Spartokori and Cookson walking their mounts behind me.

Beyond the head of the line, when we were two-thirds of the way through, there was a long open stretch between us and the next hill and now, peering ahead beyond the dust and the heat coming around that next hill, I glimpsed another pair of riders and heard the Greek mutter, "Saddle tramps."

They were coming straight toward us, no doubt about that. The one in the lead wore bull-hide chaps, the floppy brim of his horse-thief hat pinned to the crown with a cactus thorn. His companion looked meaner than gar soup thickened with tadpoles behind a scraggle of whiskers and one eye hidden behind a black patch.

"Howdy," the first one hailed as his horse passed Snude's.

The banker, ignoring him, rode straight on but Black Patch, kneeing his sorry nag in front of the girl, brought the rest of our bunch to a stop. In a quiet broken only by saddle screech and the tinkle of danglers attached to Quintada's spurs, I heard Black Patch say with a leer, "What's your hurry, hon? How's about lightin' down an' chattin' a while? These yere hills. . . ."

"Could," Schroeder's voice cut him off, "be a damn' good place to get buried in. You ever think about that?"

47

I saw Black Patch rock back in his saddle, saw the smirk on his face turn into a sneer as he looked Schroeder over with a belligerent stare. "Says who?" he jeered with a hand curled around the butt of his pistol.

"You got exactly ten seconds," Schroeder drawled soft as silk, "to get that crowbait out of our way."

For a very short moment Black Patch hung undecided then, considerably short of the time span allowed, he backed his nag to one side and we went past the pair without further words. The only one of our outfit that bothered to look back was Serafina, and you couldn't hardly miss the fright that had hold of her. Even through the sound of plodding hoofs and the rhythmic creaking of leather, I could hear the long breath that came out of Cookson, and Spartokori saying "That was a pretty near thing."

Chapter Seven

A MOUNTAIN OF ROCKS

Their feelings of relief, to my way of thinking, were considerably premature. I'd have given long odds we had not seen the last of that hard-jawed pair. The gall of that black-patched clown putting on such a play in the face of well-armed and superior numbers suggested to me there'd be others of their stripe not too far away. To me the whole incident smacked of a test. The only part that surprised me was that Schroeder hadn't shot that rascal dead in his tracks.

About an hour later, in the midst of another trough between the hills that held no sign of water, Snude pulled up and told Quintada to get the packs off and set up camp. A glance at my shadow indicated there were still several hours of daylight left, and Spartokori wanted to know if Snude figured it was safe.

"Safe for what?"

"Well, that pair of brushpoppers might have friends in this vicinity."

Bob Cookson said, "I'm not one to cry wolf, but supposing that pair decides to pay us another visit?"

"What are you . . . some kind of freak?"

Cookson flushed but held his ground. "I think those two will be back for an encore. We better be prepared. If you're bound to camp here, I think two of us, anyway, ought to stand guard."

When Bob, under Snude's embarrassing scrutiny, failed to back off, the banker said, "Fine. You've just been elected."

Cookson refused to yield an inch. He said with considerable

spirit, "I don't intend to be one of those persons who've failed to come out of this graveyard of dreams. Camping in this passage requires a guard at either side."

Schroeder, nodding, said, "I'll watch one side of this two-way trap."

Snude's cheeks darkened. Before he could get up the spit to say more, Spartokori, who'd been told to put up the girl's tent and had been pawing through the pile of equipment, wheeled to grumble at our prime mover: "Thought we had a crowbar in this stuff."

"What do you want with a crowbar?"

"I can't drive stakes into this kind of ground. I got to have something to get through this shale."

"Well, it's there some place. . . ."

"Look for yourself," Spartokori said stubbornly, still tossing things around.

"Watch out how you handle that blasting powder!" Snude yelled in alarm. With his face taking on the hue of a thunder cloud, he strode irascibly over like he was minded to ram the jimmy down the Greek's throat.

"You can't make holes with that half-ass bar!" Spartokori growled testily as Snude picked up the jimmy.

But of course there wasn't any crowbar there. I'd left it up in the cave rather than chance being caught coming down with it. With Snude looking around, riled as a hoot owl, Schroeder said, "Slipped out of one of those packs most likely coming down off that mountain."

With his mouth clamped shut the banker went off toward where Quintada was taking care of the mules. I wondered, sitting hard on my conscience, how many more of Snude's scathing lectures the Mexican would take before giving the old man a piece of his mind. I thought a kid would know better than to pitch a camp here. I didn't imagine, however, the pair of ridge runners

50

who'd accosted us would be planning to test their luck again this soon. But I reminded myself there were doubtless others just as unstable prowling these wastes and, as Bob had suggested, we'd be fools to sleep with both eyes closed.

Yet, the night passed without alarm. After breakfast Snude said, "I don't believe we'll find anything in these hills," and the Greek turned to stare at him in considerable astonishment.

"We haven't even done any real looking yet."

"You don't need to eat a bad egg to know it's rotten. The formation's not right. We'd just be wasting more time."

"Where do you figure we ought to go?" Schroeder asked.

Snude looked at me. "Chuck's our prospector. Let's have a word from him."

"Doubt if my notions would be any better. I don't put a heap of faith in that map, but it's supposed to show, isn't it, where the Peralta mines were at? I expect. . . ."

Serafina, without so much as the edge of a smile, declared: "It does show where the mines were located!"

"But those directions and distances don't mean a whole lot because after those quakes the ground don't look the same. You have to take that into consideration, and we've no guarantee who drew this map."

"Miguel drew it," she said with her chin stuck out. "My uncle told me he did!"

"Sure," I grinned. "But Miguel never saw those mines . . . most of them anyway. He got those descriptions from his sons, did he not?"

"Well . . . yes, I suppose so. But. . . ."

"There you are then. Might as well flip a coin and be done with it."

You could see they didn't none of them care to hear that.

Snude said thinly, "Where did you look that time I grubstaked you?"

51

"Away over east, and north of here. Up around Tortilla Mountain, not too far from that ranch I worked for. West of Fish Creek Cañon."

Snude nodded. "And didn't find a trace of color, you said."

"That's right. But that in itself doesn't mean much. I've yet to meet anyone who ever did find color in the Superstitions. However, there used to be a worked-out mine in that pile of rocks. Whatever was there, they got the whole of it. I worked the dump over without coming onto a thing."

Spartokori said, "If there was one mine there . . . ?"

"There could have been others," Quintada cried excitedly.

"Well, it's possible," I said, dubiously eyeing those avid faces.

Snude said gruffly, "Any place for a camp?"

"Plenty," I nodded, "but it's a long haul to water. Tortilla Creek's the only good water in half a day's ride. Leastways," I added, "the only good water I know about."

Schroeder asked, "How far is this mountain from where we're at?"

"Couple of miles maybe. It's not the distance. It's the kind of terrain you've got to contend with. Most of it's pretty dang rugged."

"Worse than Peralta Cañon?" our mule man asked.

"Well, it's not any better."

"What's two miles?" Snude said with a snort.

Spartokori growled, "I vote we take a look at it."

I said, "You've no idea what you'd be getting into. We'd have some way to get across two cañons and one hell of a lot of broken-up rock."

"At least," Cookson said, "we'd be rid of those rascals we bumped into yesterday."

"Maybe," I told him. "Wouldn't want to bet on it. This country's like a magnet to rannies run out of other places . . . kind of hellions who get their pictures in post offices, generally

52

found under the word 'Reward' or 'Wanted.' "

"I don't imagine," Snude said with curled lip, "they'll be anxious to tackle a well-armed group big as ours."

"Still," Bob Cookson said uneasily, "it's pretty well known that more than a few who've come into these mountains have just plain disappeared. . . ."

Like he was sizing up horses, Snude looked us over. "Well, partners, what's your pleasure? If you want to pull out . . . right now's the time to say so."

A pretty smooth customer, I thought to myself. Put like that no one who had red blood in his veins was going to stand up to be counted.

The Greek, looking around, said, "I vote we head for Tortilla Mountain," and one by one the rest signified agreement — even Serafina.

You may remember I'd come to this territory from the great and sovereign state of Texas in the traumatic shock of discovering my Mexican mother lying lifeless on the steps of our claim shack, with just beyond her the crouched shape of a man with a smoking pistol. A sight, I guess, that would stay with me forever, as would the face of that *pistolero*. I'd been suspicious of Schroeder ever since he'd bought chips in Snude's once-a-month poker sessions. But I couldn't be sure he was the man with the gun. In some ways it seemed he just about had to be, yet there were differences too — hardly to be wondered at, considering the years that lay between me and Texas.

Most of my schooling I'd got from my mother, a college graduate. My Irish father had more blarney than sense, a charming ineffectual provider, the bulk of whose time was spent in *cantinas* when not packing up to discover the fortune always waiting just beyond the next hill. Mother, like my old man, had a real fondness for tongue-twisting words, the more syllables packed into them the greater her enjoyment — about the only real joy she had,

I expect. This high-flown vocabulary, I'd often thought, was the most substantial part of my inheritance and, though I'd done my best and had shed a good part of it, those two-dollar words were still occasionally cropping up, the bane of my existence in the cow camps.

Once they'd pinned down our destination, Cookson assisting Quintada got the packs on the mules and little time was lost in getting under way. With myself in the lead we quit the Red Hills and struck out for that great heap of rocks some fool in the past had labeled Tortilla Mountain. It made about as much sense as my old man's travels. I'd have given long odds they'd find nothing there.

It took us half the day to get ourselves and our animals down into La Barge Cañon, tempers getting shorter with every step and stumble, Black Mountain darkly frowning on our efforts off to the left. Another hour was spent trying to get our transport up the opposite slope, with sheer cliffs and rock slides forcing us to detour along precarious goat trails, not counting the times we had to backtrack.

When we finally got out on level ground, with Music Mountain a whoop and a holler off to our right and that damned pile of broken rocks we were bound for falsely looming near enough to spit on, there wasn't one in our outfit that wasn't plumb bushed.

With a huge sigh of relief Snude exclaimed, eyeing it, "Let's hustle up and get over there."

I gave him a pitying look and said grimly, "Unless you can flop your flippers and fly, you're not going to get there before tomorrow night. We've still got Peter's Cañon ahead of us, a rock-ribbed narrow bitch of a slit we'll be most of tomorrow getting into and out of."

"I'm pooped," Cookson sighed. "Let's camp right here and get some grub under our belts."

It seemed as good a place as we were likely to find, without water of course, but there was plenty of room for our livestock and piñons affording dead wood for our fire, so I seconded his notion. With the rest too bone weary to argue, Quintada was told to get the packs off the mules.

You had to admire that Peralta female. All through this grueling, monstrous trip, with the rest of them griping their heads off, not once did Serafina open her mouth — about the only good thing I can find to say about what we were doing.

With our supplies unloaded and Cookson breaking off dead limbs for his fire, I helped Quintada feed and water the animals. Except for its obvious lack of moisture this spread-out level with its fringe of woods offered about as much comfort as we were likely to find. Once the fire was blazing cheerfully, I noticed Bob Cookson getting out the big pot. Convinced of his intention when he dumped half the contents of his water bag into it, I had to dig through my store of private cuss words to fetch up one that could begin to do justice to the meals I saw ahead of us. When I saw him upend a sack of whistleberries into it, I knew for sure we were about to be treated to the cowhand's delight.

When, after a supper of boiled beans and Bob's petrified biscuits, the rest of us sought our blankets, Snude at my urging and just to be on the safe side elected Schroeder to patrol the camp's confines as guard against possible intruders. But the night passed quietly again, without anything more disturbing than a big cat's howls.

After a skimpy breakfast of fried beans and sowbelly, we got the mules once more under their packs and took off for Peter's Cañon. As the crow flies, it was less than a mile straight ahead. It was close to noon when we finally dropped into it and, discovering no way of climbing out at this point, the whole outfit munching on jerky in lieu of a meal, we set off single file through its shimmering heat and torturous twists in a muttering quest for some means of getting out. In this arduous fashion, with the sun-baked slopes of Music Mountain hovering over our shoulders, we must have toiled south the worst part of a mile before finding a place the mules and horses could tackle. And then, of course, we had to work our way back across the rock-cluttered footslopes to our objective through the lengthening shadows.

On one of these slopes in a grove of live oak promising welcome shade during the blistering heat of whatever days Snude decided to spend prowling the mountain, we made our base camp not far from the west bank of Tortilla Creek. After a disgusting supper of refried beans pieced out with more of Cookson's hard-as-rock biscuits, the whole outfit repaired to the creek for a much needed bath in the dark before moonrise. Serafina meandered upstream a ways to make sure she wouldn't be furnishing a spectacle.

Later, while the rest appeared far enough out of earshot, Spartokori took the opportunity as he was passing my bedroll to ask rather plaintively, "You reckon His Nibs knows what the hell he's doin' out here?"

I grinned up at him. "Expect, anyway, he knows enough about gold not to lug home a bunch of pyrites."

The Greek let go of his breath in a snort and, shoving hands in his pockets, moved off toward the fire. Though I had more on my mind than a man could keep track of, I was so damn' weary I went to sleep straightaway.

For breakfast we got corned beef and what was left of Bob's biscuits. We had another bright sunshiny day ahead of us. While Quintada was saddling four of the horses, Schroeder, getting off his butt, came over to ask if I honestly thought we would get anywhere stumbling around on that mountain. I said I didn't think so and Snude, already mounted, peering off toward the nearest rock-strewn slope, demanded to be shown the abandoned mine I had mentioned.

He said, "We can't all go and leave this stuff unguarded. Since you're the best shot in our outfit, Schroeder, why don't you stay in camp along with Serafina and our wrangler. Okay?"

"Suits me."

Serafina nodded, apparently glad for a bit of rest. Spartokori, saying he'd like a look at that cave, swung onto his horse. Cookson and me each climbed into leather and the four of us set off.

From where we had camped we had a pretty clear view of this side of the mountain and a considerable amount of relatively open country between us and it grown to clumps of juniper wherever the rocky soil allowed a purchase. The old Spanish Trail was still discernible a good way up the slope. I pointed this out to the others. It was a lot steeper climb getting up to it than had appeared from below. By the time we reached it we had to pause a few minutes to let our horses catch up with their breaths.

"Pretty stiff going," Cookson commented, and I assured him he hadn't seen anything yet.

"Where's the cave?" the Greek asked.

"The mine's a couple of rope lengths away from the crown and the cave's just below. Some thirty or forty feet if I remember."

"Well, let's get at it," Snude said impatiently.

A short time after we'd put our mounts into motion again, I said: "Expect we better do the rest of this afoot. We're about to get into a lot of loose rock that's weathered off the crown — bad place for horses."

Bob inquired, "How's this place for snakes?"

"I only saw two last time I was up here. Don't imagine we'll see any."

So we left the horses on grounded reins and tackled the remainder of the climb on shanks' mare. It was pretty rugged work. Getting over those fallen rocks was no task for dudes. The first bit of carelessness could almighty easy result in a broken leg or ankle, a foregone conclusion that didn't bear thinking of. We were still, as I saw looking over my shoulder, not over a hundred yards above our tail-switching horses with double that distance still to go. Because of the way the rocks lay, we couldn't climb straight up but were forced to angle back and forth across the face of this slope in order to bypass the worst of the obstructions.

We had to take time out to get back our wind whenever the terrain permitted. Crawling over and around and between those great chunks of shattered rock in full glare of the sun, now directly overhead, was a real test of character and fetched a number of things to light a man wouldn't normally care to exhibit. With the sweat pouring off our faces like someone had emptied a bucket over us and with the chance every minute of breaking our necks, the only reason more foul language wasn't heard was we scarcely had enough breath left to grunt with.

With the cave not more than ten yards above me, I stopped to have a look at how the others were faring. Farthest off — a good rope's length behind — was Cookson, just standing in his sweat, braced against an upthrust slab, puffing like an engine on the Santa Fe. Scarcely three strides above him was Spartokori, looking pretty near done in. The only one even reasonably close, and this surprised me, was the sunburnt Ebbert Snude.

My throat was dry as an old bleached bone. "You fellows want to quit?" I managed to get out as I stood waiting. Somebody swore. No one else said anything. I nodded toward a ledge that stuck out above me. I said, "That's where the cave is," and they all bent over and started climbing again.

I waited on the ledge, glad to sit down with my legs dangling over it. One after another they all came up and collapsed alongside of me, even Snude whose view of himself as president of Tucson's biggest bank was no longer sharp enough to cope with what that climb had taken out of him. But he was first one up with an affronted look to demand, resentful and packed with impatience, that I show him the mine.

"You can't miss it," I said, "if you go straight up. That's the dump right above us. Just watch out for rattlers."

Without further words he set off to have a look at it. I don't know what he expected to find. It was just an empty, untimbered hole some fool had dug into the face of the mountain. It only went in about twenty feet before the digger had concluded he was wasting his time.

"Let's get into this cave," Spartokori said presently, getting onto his feet.

"That mine really played out?" Bob asked.

"Near as I been able to make out, it was nothing but rock from one end to the other," I said. "I can't believe there's a nickel's worth of ore any place on this mountain."

"Then what was the point in us ever coming up here?" Cookson grumbled, looking like he wanted to throw away the jimmy he had hooked to his belt.

"Well, you heard Snude. He was bound and determined to have a look at that hole. And you," I said, glancing round at the Greek, "were busting to see the inside of the cave. A handful of shards from some long-forgotten pot and a few bits of flint is about all the good it's likely to do you."

We followed the Greek inside. The light of his torch went over the floor to show, as I'd told them, the place was empty.

Bob, looking about, asked, "How well did you go over this?"

"How long does it take to show an empty cave's empty?"

But Cookson was already tapping the nearest wall with the crook of his jimmy.

Spartokori with his brows up asked, "What's he looking for?

59

A hidden room?"

I shrugged, picturing the cache we'd clandestinely uncovered on Bluff Spring Mountain.

The Greek went on watching Cookson, listening like myself to the sound of Bob's tapping. So far, at least, it appeared to be wasted effort.

With an air of concentration, still tapping, Bob was moving now toward the back of the cave, pausing abruptly to run a hand across the wall directly ahead of him. He glanced at me over his shoulder and I caught the acquisitive glint in his stare before, turning away, he resumed his search. Very shortly his tapping produced a different timbre.

"Sounds hollow," the Greek muttered, leaning forward, eyes narrowing.

Bob moved half a step to his right, still tapping, still producing this new hollow resonance. Spartokori appeared nearly excited as he was. Still tapping, Bob said, "When I was a kid, I was never so happy as the night before Christmas, poking at the packages under the tree. You'd think, by rights, I should have become a prospector. There's nothing I like better than turning up something other folks have missed."

"When I was a kid," Spartokori remarked, "I got two apples and a orange stuffed into my sock" — and looked around at me. "Reckon there's something back of that wall?"

"If there is, we've got a problem."

The watermelon sound had stopped following Bob's thumps. He stopped tapping and faced us.

"Do we bring in Snude to share whatever's waiting back of this wall, or do we quit right here and postpone the grand opening until we three can come back and keep it all for ourselves? As our banker would say, 'What's your pleasure, gents?' "

Chapter Eight

COOKSON SPEAKS HIS MIND

Greedy and devious, I thought, staring at him, and clever besides, leaving us with the onus of making the decision.

The Greek's agonized expression showed him tugged two ways. In the refracted light from his torch I could see the shine of sweat breaking out on him. He was busting to know what was back of that wall, but too many years of driving hard bargains made it near impossible for him to consider additional partners sharing what Bob had just put us next to. I caught a glimpse of the amusement bubbling back of Cookson's black, watching stare and could almost sympathize with the Greek's dilemma.

Spartokori's tongue moved across dry lips. With a kind of groan, he grumbled, "I pass."

So the choice fell on me, and I was about to say I was willing to share when a sudden and newly found distrust of Bob — or perhaps it was just his trying to maneuver us — made me say, "Believe I'll pass, too." His mouth tightened angrily behind the black beard. "Hoist with your own petard," I chuckled. And could see at once that for all his intelligence, humor was something not included in his perceptions.

Quick to hide his discomfort, he said with just a bit less than his usual adroitness, "Whichever way we're about to jump, we've all got to jump in the same direction. Makes sense, doesn't it?"

Spartokori, still plainly disgruntled, jerked his head in a nod. I said flatly, "Ambiguous is what it looks like to me."

He sidestepped this. "In the world of ideas," he pontificated

61

dryly, "we sometimes come across an occasional jasper that has to be hit over the head with a notion before his wits get to working."

The Greek looked at me, "What the hell's he talkin' about?"

"Just runnin' off at the mouth," I said. "Hadn't we better go up and see what's keeping Snude?"

Spartokori said, "Go on if you want. I've had all the climbin' I can stomach today."

"Me, too," Bob allowed with that hint of a smile I found so exasperating.

So with nothing settled one way or the other, we all went out and hunkered down on the ledge. While the others were busied with tobacco sacks and papers, I looked over the country spread out below and wondered what was keeping Snude up there so long. Serafina's tent showed me where our camp was, but I could see no sign of movement, either there or in that vicinity.

What I did see, and it gave me a turn, was dust some four-five miles north of us drifting south along the old Spanish Trail. It was the sort of dust stirred up by horsebackers and what bothered me most — whoever this might turn out to be — was the fact that this trail crossed the slope just below where we'd left our ground-hitched horses.

I jogged Cookson's elbow and jerked my chin toward the approaching dust.

He caught on straightaway — wasn't anything slow about Bob's wits. "One of us better get down there."

Spartokori, craning his neck, said, "What's up?"

"Company coming."

"That's bad?"

"Could be damn' bad if they spot that tent or make off with our horses."

"Who you think it could be?"

Cookson said, "You're better getting over these rocks than we are, Chuck. . . ."

With no time to waste and knowing already where that talk was pointed, I got off my butt and headed for the horses, wishing I had the rifle I'd left on my saddle.

Halfway to the horses I looked again for that dust and could see this was about to be another near thing. It was plain now there were two of them coming along at an easy lope, maybe two miles away. I could see our mounts, with cocked ears, watching their progress.

It was no easy chore, across that rock-cluttered slope, getting down to the horses ahead of that pair and I pretty nearly didn't. Where we'd left our mounts wasn't more than fifty yards above where that trail was going to take those buggers past us. I had just got my saddle gun clear of leather when Black Patch yelled up to me.

"Prospectin', are you?"

"No, we're just climbin' around for the sunshine."

"You found that Dutchman's mine yet?" the one in the bull-hide chaps asked sardonically.

I was standing with my horse between them and me by deliberate precaution and with the barrel of my rifle comfortably resting across the saddle. Finger hooked around the trigger, I told them, "Don't want to seem impolite, understand, but if you're goin' somewhere, don't let me detain you."

"Oh," Bull-Hide Chaps said, "we ain't in no hurry. Always got time to shoot the breeze with old friends."

"You've got no friends here. And, speakin' of shootin', I got a damn' itchy trigger finger."

Black Patch said, "Kinda tetchy, ain't he?"

"Tetchy as a god-damned snake," Bull-Hide Chaps decided. "Must 'a' been raised on panther piss."

"All right, you two . . . hit the trail," I growled. "Clear out before I do you a hurt."

"You reckon he could?" Bull-Hide Chaps asked in pretended alarm.

"Naw. Looks like to me he's jest got a big mouth. . . ."

He quit his monkeyshines, startled, when the bang of my rifle took the hat off his head. He made a wild grab, barely managing to catch it, put spurs to his critter like the heel flies were at him, the burly one in the chaps crowding to get his hide out of range. I watched their departure for another five minutes in no way deceived by their clowning.

When Snude with the others came scrambling down to join me, Spartokori growled, "You was lucky as hell them two didn't clobber you!"

I said, "No luck about it. Man with the drop generally has the last word. Before we're much older that pair will be back."

"What do you reckon they're up to?" Bob asked.

"No good, that's for sure." I said to Snude, "You find anything up there?"

The banker shook his head. "Just an old empty hole."

He was a pretty good dissembler. I guessed he'd had a heap of practice. It was dang unlikely, I told myself, he'd been staring at an empty hole all that time. His look of disgust didn't put me off.

Tagging along behind Spartokori as Snude, who was well ahead, led the way back to camp, I dropped back part way down to let Cookson catch up with me. First thing he said was, "What do you reckon he got onto up there?"

"Whatever it was I should have seen it myself unless something's been left there since I went over it. The hole, when I was in there, came up against solid rock. I pawed through the dump, like I told him, and never found so much as a hint of color."

"How big around was that hole at the end of it?"

"Not very damn big."

"All right. Supposing what you took for solid rock was, in fact, a boulder?"

"I guess it could have been. Looked just like the hole all around it. Guess one of us should've gone up there with him. What you got in mind?"

"The walls of that cave, leastways the ones I was tapping, looked solid enough, too . . . not the ghost of a seam or a crack any place. Yet we got a different sound when I was thumping that one part. Both of you reckoned, same as me, there was a hollow place back of it, a pretty good sized one, maybe a room. Right?"

"I'll go along with that."

"So how did it get there? You know what I think?" he said, probing my face. "Nobody went through that wall I was tapping. Suppose one of them old Spaniards, or some of those long-gone Apaches, stumbled onto that hole some gopherin' prospector left behind and aimed to hide something they didn't want found . . . ?"

"Like what?"

"You've likely heard as many stories as I have. Those Peraltas and their peons knew the Indians were fed up with them. Lots of people have disappeared around here and all of their belongings. Must've been plenty of loot over the years." Bob spoke avidly. "Somebody dug that barren hole. Someone else stumbled onto it . . . lot of people, maybe. I'll bet somebody reaching the end of that tunnel done some more digging."

"You think Snude discovered that rock could be moved?"

"Not only that. I think he moved it."

"And got into that hollow behind the cave wall?"

"He never spent all that time up there saying his prayers!"

More food for thought and, perhaps, a better insight into what made Cookson so outrageously successful in a country where business mostly leaned toward cattle and what was concerned with them. And he could well be right in his assumptions about Snude. The man had been up there a good deal longer than it took to stare at an empty hole. If Bob was right, it would seem Snude had no intention of sharing his knowledge.

Was the real purpose of this trip not so much to hunt lost mines as to give him an opportunity, with our protection, to have a look at that hole? It seemed absurd. But if it *wasn't* his notion — the larger the party, the less interference you'd be likely to run into — why had he roped us into this? It was hardly probable we'd been fetched along with the idea of sharing anything of value we might happen to turn up.

Such thoughts might be doing Snude a grave injustice but, in view of his reputation as a man who'd skin a flea, I didn't believe it. He hadn't got where he was by doing unto others the way he'd like to be done to.

The shank of the afternoon had crept up on us practically unnoticed, with the evening shadows stretching long and dark across the grass clumps and rabbit brush as we rode into camp, cheered by the supper smells drifting above Serafina's pot-hung fire. She was one of our outfit of whom I could thoroughly approve.

I wished now I had scrutinized Snude more closely when he'd come down to where I'd been holding the horses after watching the departure of those two uglies. If, as Cookson thought, he'd found a way into that hollow behind the cave wall, there might have been rock dust clinging to his clothes. If the end of that tunnel had been no more than a boulder and he'd found how to move it, once displaced he'd have had to wriggle through the aperture. Any exercise of this nature would almost certainly have left some marks. He showed no evidence of that now. In the usual high-and-mighty fashion he believed indigenous to a man of his status, he lost no time in telling Quintada to take care of our livestock and, when that was finished, to break up some more dead branches for the fire.

Serafina had fixed us a meal of rabbit stew with dumplings and a dried-apple pie to top it off. She had real culinary talent and brewed the best coffee with which I ever washed down grub.

On account of those two vagrants, Snude had made up his mind to post guards again that night and declared he and I would take the first shift. When the rest had sought their blankets, he told me where I should take up my vigil, which was where I could keep one eye on our animals and the other on the lookout for any intruders who might come pussyfooting around. After giving me an encouraging nod, he went stalking off to the camp's farthest perimeter and into some covert where the tree-casts shadow appeared to be blackest. Winchester ready across my knees, I put my back to a still-warm rock and hoped I could manage to stay awake.

Looking out across the moonlit range leading up to the mountain and its footslope where the four of us had spent this muscle-stretching day, I tried to recall if Snude in any fashion had at any time attempted to steer us toward this particular peak. It didn't seem likely we had been so manipulated. It appeared, in looking back on our erratic course and its several changed directions, more probably the gyrations of a man unable to make up his mind.

I reckoned Snude twice as old as any of us but Schroeder. I recalled my mother's explaining my father's dilatory behavior as being due primarily to a malady "which appears to attack most men of his years," she'd said. "An eroding of the intellect."

It was hard to see this as a likely explanation of Ebbert Snude's puzzling antics. I'd a pretty good hunch anything he did was done with 'malice aforethought,' for some concealed but deliberate purpose. I simply couldn't believe an impulsive man could have got to be president of Beach & Bascomb's Commercial Bank.

Nor could I think some random impulse or hobbyish enthusiasm was responsible for this venture into what had become known as the "killer mountains."

So wrapped up had I become in these notions, I'd no idea I was not alone in my vigil till I felt the touch of a hand on my shoulder. With a guilty start I spun to stare at the recognizable shape of Serafina, diaphanous in night clothes. Barefoot she was, which may have explained how she had managed to elude my hearing.

"I must talk with you," she whispered. "Where's Snude?"

"Over there some place under the trees. You know," I muttered, worriedly keeping my voice down, "you shouldn't be out here like this."

"Ho!" she said, brushing that aside. "I have to discuss with you something, and this is the first chance I've had to get you alone. What is Snude up to? What are we doing here?"

"We're supposed to be hunting the Peralta mines. He said you were with us on account of the map you got from Gonzales. Big trouble is, as I've said before, that map was made before those quakes shook up this country. Things don't look any more like they did in your uncle's time."

"After that first day he hardly looked at it."

"Well," I said, "it don't seem to make much sense probably because most of the landmarks it mentions . . . the essential ones . . . are no longer visible."

"The map doesn't show anything on this mountain, nor does it show a Peralta mine near that first mountain we camped on." Crouched there in the moonlight, her eyes were wide and searching, as though I must know what all this was about. "I can't understand him. When we discussed this at the bank, he seemed so kind and wanting to be helpful. Now, he hardly looks at the map and pays no attention to me at all. Except," she added in a frightened sort of tone, "whenever I'm talking to someone

68

else, I find him watching like a cat at a mouse hole."

"Have you told him something he's been keeping to himself? I mean, some inside tip he hasn't shared with the rest of us? Some secret or hunch Gonzales passed on to you?"

"I know of nothing like that. So far as I'm aware, the only real secret the Peraltas were concerned with was the locations of their mines and those, my uncle said, were revealed on the map he gave me."

"Did he mention why he'd not personally put that knowledge to use . . . why he hadn't come back here?"

"Several of the mines, he said, had played out, gone into barren rock, and he felt this country was too dangerous."

"Because of the Apaches?"

She shrugged. "He said he had thought of returning when the gringo government took over this country but had not done so 'because of the risk.' "

I could not quite see what risk could have persuaded him to turn his back, figuratively speaking, on a source of guaranteed wealth. "Was Gonzales well off?"

"I've always heard that the Peraltas of Sonora lived like kings, that they were persons of great influence and vast estates. But Gonzales, as I remember him, was old and stooped and walked with a cane. He lived at that time in Tucson's Mexican working-class quarter in one of those old adobe houses on Meyer Street. What he had, actually, was no more than a room in the house of José Quintada."

"Quintada!"

When that exclamation jumped out of me, the grip she had on my arm squeezed tighter. "Yes . . . I thought about that. But our Quintada, when I asked about it, denied any relationship to the Meyer Street Quintadas . . . said his folks all lived in Guadalajara."

This did not surprise me. He would hardly care in his present

69

situation to have Snude discover any connection between him and the people with whom Gonzales had spent his last days.

"Did he seem upset when you questioned him?"

She shook her head. "Not at all." She added, plainly worried, "I wish I knew what to think about him."

"Snude, you mean?"

"He seems such a secretive person. . . ."

"You ever know a banker who wasn't?"

"I've never met any bankers other than him."

"Probably just as well off. I think he's here on a fishing expedition . . . wants a look at the country."

"He seemed different when I spoke with him in Tucson. Attentive, friendly, seemed quite anxious to help. . . ."

"Do you reckon he'd found out you had Miguel's map?"

"Yes, I told him I had this map Gonzales had given me along with a piece of the Peralta ore."

"You didn't show him the map?"

She shook her head. "I showed him the piece of ore. . . ."

"Just a minute," I broke in. "Was . . . would you say the piece of ore he saw was like all the rest of the Peralta ore?"

"I have an idea it wasn't. It came, my uncle said, from the Number Four Mine, one of those, I believe, that ran into *borrasca*. I guess Snude didn't think to ask about that. What I wanted to know was how to go about relocating the Peralta mines. He said it was possible he might put together a company of equal partners to put up the considerable finances involved in such a venture if that would be agreeable, all sharing alike in whatever we turned up."

"And you agreed to be robbed of the bulk of your inheritance?"

She said, after a moment, "I wasn't quite that foolish. I said I imagined I could do better than that and reached for my specimen. He looked tremendously astonished and remarked that I would not find it easy to interest competent and trustworthy persons to take on such a gamble. He finally agreed I would be given two shares and fixed up the papers himself while I stayed there and watched our signatures being notarized."

"When did he get his first look at the map?"

"He would need my sample, he said, to show the investors, so I let him have it. But it wasn't until just before we started that I allowed him to examine Don Miguel's map."

"Guess we'll just have to make the best of it," I nodded, thinking what a rascal this banker really was. The mines revealed on the map were numbered, but what descriptions I'd been able to find only took in the more pertinent mountains, none of these showing the names they bore today. And she'd been wrong in thinking there was no Peralta mine on the mountain I was staring at over her shoulder. I said, "Your Number Four specimen looks remarkably like the ore Jake Walzer brought out of these mountains. And your present companions are the competent investors Snude found. Who among them can you trust . . . *if* we find anything . . . not to gobble it all?"

"I can trust you, can't I?"

The expression on her face was hard to read with all that moonlight behind her.

"I hope so," I mumbled, and saw the shape of her stiffen.

She let go of my arm and stepped back a pace. "Don't think I can't take care of myself. I have a pistol" — she said this with a lift of her chin — "and I know how to use it!"

I pulled in a long breath, thinking back on that cave and the tunnel above it. "Good. Keep it handy . . . and watch out for snakes."

71

Chapter Nine

THE NUMBER FOUR MINE

Staring off into the moon-silvered night, recalling the way she had slipped through the shadows graceful as an antelope, making no more sound than a scalp-hunting Apache, I considered myself with considerable disgust. Who was I to fling rocks at the rest of them? A bugger quite ready to skin his partners for hidden gain so long as they didn't get next to him.

I remembered the cache on Bluff Spring Mountain and Bob fiercely crying as we eyed our plunder: "Well . . . the hell with them! We're not obligated to share this with them!" I should have spoken up right then and not waited to be shown by Serafina the kind of turd I was turning into.

Filled with revulsion I peered across the fire's dying embers at that bitch of a mountain and saw myself as she must have seen me, glad the dark had hidden her face when she'd sprung back to mention that pistol.

The scuff of a step hauled my head around sharply, rifle lifting in startled hands.

"For Christ's sake, Chuck! It's only me," Spartokori gulped, stepping into my sight.

I lowered the rifle. "Is it your turn already?"

"Hell, no! I'd just like to know what you think of this deal and why Snude was up in that tunnel so long. I been going over and over it in my head an' getting no place."

"Hell," I said, "you got plenty of company. The girl was just here wantin' to know what he's up to. . . ."

"I figure he put together this trip to see how the land lay."

"You don't think he's hunting Walzer's mine?"

"That too, of course. I think he's looking for gold in one form or another. I've been in that tunnel. What I took to be solid rock back there at the end of it might have been a movable boulder . . . that's what Bob thinks. Now suppose, poking around, Snude managed to move it and found himself starin' at more tunnel behind it?"

"That hollow place back of the cave wall. You reckon he's been into it?"

"I don't see how unless there is more tunnel than I've seen. It would have to dip and turn at right angles, which is certainly possible. If there is, and it does, there may have been a mine up here after all and in spite of that map."

Spartokori said rather grimly, "You reckon there was?"

"My guess would be no better than yours. But whoever drew that map . . . somebody, anyway, put numbers on the mines and there's no Number Four." In the dark of those shadows we stared at each other, the Greek slowly nodding.

I said, "According to the girl, that piece of Peralta ore Snude showed us came from the Number Four Mine."

"That does it," he growled, staring up at the mountain. "We better go up there. If there's a mine, Snude's been into it, you can be damn' sure of that!"

"Maybe. But there's something else you can also be sure of: if I go up to that tunnel, it won't be at night. Those rocks're not the kind to be crawled over in the dark."

We eyed each other some more. Then Spartokori said, "If he wasn't such a bastard, we could ask him straight out."

"Let it ride for a bit. At least until we see what he's got on tap for tomorrow."

After he went off to try again to get some sleep, I kept going over the whole thing in my head. A good part of this thinking made no sense at all. I thought in the uneasy silence that, if Snude told us in the morning we might as well pack up and get out of here, it didn't take a crystal ball to foresee there was likely to be trouble.

Staring off across the rabbit brush and broomweeds, it occurred to me these were all an Apache would need to creep up on this camp, not that I imagined any were out there. Most of the Indians these days were living in towns or on the reservation guzzling beer and dreaming of better times. But this was no country for a man to be careless in.

Damned near any place you looked, there'd be a mountain whose upper reaches afforded ample concealment and a ready-made lookout for persons wanting to spy on other people's business. And some of these hellions might be peering at us now. I hadn't forgotten that pair of footloose drifters. Range tramps, someone had called them. The sort that, given a chance, would make buzzard bait out of you for what they could get out of your pockets or for the horse you had under you. Not the kind of thought a man would care to take to bed with him.

Quintada showed up to take over my vigil. He said Schroeder had gone to relieve Snude of his. The last thought I had, settling into my soogans with a cold wind whipping down off the peaks, was of the lone girl we had in our midst.

In the morning, halfway through one of Bob's lousy breakfasts with the sun not yet peeking over the crags, Snude surprised us.

"There's a mine on that mountain," he said, looking round at us. "I think we may be onto something. We'll stay here a while and have a good look at it."

Serafina seemed astonished. Spartokori and myself did our best to follow suit. Quintada eyed him over a dropped jaw. Schroeder's was the only face that didn't show anything.

Cookson said, "You're putting us on."

74

Snude grinned. "Not at all. Chuck must have looked that place over with his eyes shut. The lumpy rock where the tunnel appeared to end is a carefully fitted boulder balanced on a very ingenious pivot. There's more tunnel behind it, much wider and high enough to stand straight up in. Knowing you boys were probably getting impatient that's as far as I went. . . ."

"Then," Schroeder said, "how do you know it's a mine?"

"Because, flashing my torch on the walls, I could see the stringers of gold winking back at me. You'll be able to see for yourselves when we go up there."

"How come you said nothing about this yesterday?" Spartokori growled.

I said, "Reckon he wanted us to get a good night's sleep."

"That's right," the banker nodded. "Plenty of time today to look it over when we can see how to get up there without breaking any legs. Someone's got to keep an eye on our animals and Serafina. . . ."

"Serafina," she said, looking him straight in the eye, "stayed in camp yesterday."

"Getting up on that mountain's pretty hazardous work," Cookson told her, and got a scornful look.

"As majority stockholder in this enterprise," she announced with an edge of belligerence, "I intend to look after my interests. When do you figure to start?" she asked Snude.

"Soon as. . . ."

"I'm ready right now," Spartokori growled with a look at me. "Chuck thought. . . ."

"When you took so long up at that hole," I said hastily, "we figured you might be settin' up stakes to take over the whole top of the mountain."

Snude laughed. "Any stakes set up will be in joint ownership." Then he said with a thoughtful stare roving over my face, "I'm not even sure we should stake this claim till we can fetch enough men up there to hold it. What do you think, Chuck?"

"What you saw in those walls may be all there is. There's also the question of what to do about those two rannies we saw in the Red Hills. Now that they've followed us over here, I think it might be a good idea to stay away from that mountain, at least till we're sure they're not hangin' around."

None of them, apparently, agreed with that notion. I hung onto my patience till they ran out of breath. "We don't know," I said then, "how many more of their sort are keepin' tabs on us."

Snude took a look at the roundabout peaks. "Chuck could be right, you know. He's had some acquaintance. . . ."

"He just might be acquainted," Schroeder said, "with them."

I looked at him sourly. "All who believe that should have their heads looked at."

Bob Cookson chuckled. But the rest I thought — even Serafina — were looking at me with varying degrees of speculation, almost as though I was a two-headed calf.

"That's right," I said, "they might be part of my *corrida*," but only Cookson grinned. The girl appeared almost as shocked as Spartokori. It occurred to me I'd have done a lot better to have kept my mouth shut.

The complete stillness following my misguided attempt at satire showed how little real humor I could look for in this outfit. Then all of them began chattering like a bunch of catbirds on the same branch.

Stopping in mid-sentence, Serafina threw up both hands. "You can't really believe such a preposterous notion? Why, I'd stake my life on Chuck's integrity!"

They were still staring at me when Schroeder allowed, "It could happen. That's not as farfetched as you think."

I kept my lip hobbled.

Snude said abruptly, "Now we've had our little joke, we better give some serious thought to what we're going to do about those two uglies. Like Chuck said, considering the way they've been doggin' our tracks, it's certainly possible they've got friends in this vicinity. If they should run off our animals, we could be in bad shape."

"So what's your solution?" Cookson asked.

Appearing to turn that over, Snude said soberly, "I guess three of us anyway will have to stick around camp at all times till we get this ironed out."

"You going to pick them?" Spartokori grumbled.

"I suppose the fairest way would be to draw straws," Snude decided in a tone that suggested he was not too happy with it.

This didn't suit Serafina, either. "I'm going," she told him, "no matter what length of straw I draw."

"Of course. That leaves two others," he nodded, breaking off five lengths from the nearest clump of grass. This decision suited nobody, least of all those who figured they would be left in camp.

Snude gave Schroeder first choice by thrusting out the hand in which nothing but the ends of the grass were showing. The next to reach for a stem was Quintada, who promptly measured his against the stem in Schroeder's fist, which just as promptly eliminated our wrangler who asked, looking stupid as only he could manage, "Which one gets to go?"

"The two longest, naturally," Schroeder grunted from an expressionless face.

I was the last to draw and was rewarded by getting the longest stem. The other long piece went to Spartokori who grinned at Cookson. "Tough luck," he said with satisfaction.

Bob shrugged but, like Quintada, watched resentfully as Snude, Serafina, Spartokori, and myself saddled up to take off. Schroeder's enigmatic stare gave no clue to what was going on behind it. As we kneed our mounts toward the slopes that gave onto the mountain, Bob called after us, "Watch your step in that tunnel!"

The sun was really bearing down by the time we reached the old Spanish Trail. Snude, peering thoughtfully back toward me, said: "Might be smart not to leave our horses where we did yesterday. What do you think, Chuck?"

I thought it a good idea and said so. "Be fair game if that pair of varmints are still hanging around."

So, turning left along the old trail, we followed him for four or five minutes, at which point he said, "Right here the climb doesn't look quite so rugged and we'll be able to take the horses farther up." He put his mount to the slope, us tagging along single file behind him. The ascent wasn't as steep here and there were fewer fallen rocks to get around. When he pulled up at the first fairly level place above one of the outcrops, glancing back I saw that we had come a good piece and were about two-thirds of the way up the mountain. The tunnel entrance was not more than a hundred yards above us.

Leaving the horses there, we set out afoot, Snude packing his water sack, the girl right behind him, then Spartokori, and me and my rifle right on his tail. Reaching the cave, we sat down on the ledge to draw in a few breaths and look back toward the camp and the animals the others had been left to guard.

We could see Serafina's tent plainly enough, the three horses and the mules, but no sign of the men.

"Probably taking a snooze," Snude said with curled lip.

I said, "I can't believe Schroeder would be that much of a fool. He strikes me as a man who's been around. I'll give odds he's got both eyes open."

"Well," Snude said, "I hope you're right," and got onto his feet. "Let's get up there. I'd like to know if what we've found is worth all the bother, all this climbing around."

The grade was considerably steeper, this last forty yards. We took another breather before crawling into that hole. Inside we were able to get on our feet again, staring in the light of Spartokori's torch at where the tunnel narrowed to come up against what I had taken to be solid rock. Serafina, anyway, and Spartokori appeared pretty excited when Snude, down on his knees, put a hand against the lower part of that barrier. We watched it swing away and, as Snude wriggled through the hole thus revealed, we saw him stand up in the much wider space beyond. Serafina wriggled through then and, after her, Spartokori. Leaving my rifle, I got down on all four and followed.

They were all looking excited as they stood staring about them at the corrugated quartz walls with their rutiles of gold glittering in the light where the picks had abandoned them no telling how many years in the past. Peering beyond my companions' elongated shadows into the dimness that concealed what lay beyond in that uncanny quiet, I had a number of uncomfortable thoughts before Snude, switching on his own torch, said, "Let's find out what we've got here."

He led the way, setting off to see where this passage would take us. It was, I thought, a lot like prospecting, never knowing till you got there what the next step might turn up. But it was also, to me, strange, weighted perhaps with premonition or some horrid foreboding as with grim reluctance I traipsed after the black shapes of my companions amid the eerily echoing crunch of booted feet moving steadily deeper into the bowels of the earth.

Warm air pulsed against my cheek from some pore in the walls where quartz gave way to barren basalt and, presently, dolamite as the tunnel burrowed its twisted way ever more disturbingly toward the innermost secrets of the slumbering mountain in its despairing effort to recover the lost vein. I shut off my torch, wanting both hands free in the untimbered passage as I followed the others through the dancing shadows of this funnel-like trek past barren rock toward an unknown destination.

We came in due course to where the narrowing walls forced us into single file as they bent abruptly to the right, back in the direction of the mountain's outer crust. Another, colder, flow of air washed over me from unseen tons of rock above as the passage widened into what had all the appearance of a lofty room whose roof was lost in the jibbering dark.

"Bats," Snude said in disgust, peering up at them.

All three of them had stopped. Against the light of Snude's torch, they looked as rigidly anchored as the shapes of cigar store Indians, speechlessly staring at tier on tier of bulging canvas sacks stacked, God knew how deep, against the unseen walls of what must once have been an overhand stope.

Spartokori was first to find his voice.

"What," he gasped, "have we got into?"

Snude, as though he were Montezuma, declared, "The store-room, of course. Judging by those quartz walls up above, I'd say we've come onto the source of Walzer's fabulous ore."

I guessed he was right. The Dutchman with his engineering background would have had the ability to have tailored and rigged that pivoted boulder, replacing whatever had originally blocked this part of the mine. Presumably, what we saw stacked up around the walls was the ore the Peraltas had mined before being forced to abandon the site in their unsuccessful flight from the Apaches who had subsequently killed them.

The Greek, darting past Snude and the girl, moved to the nearest of those bulging sacks and quick as scat ran a knife up the end one. Nothing spilled from the rent. The contents, crammed so tight through all those years by the weight of its fellows pressing down from above, appeared chunk on chunk to have grown into each other to form a solid mass.

Spartokori, swearing, grabbed a cut flap with such a yank the half rotted fabric tore off in his fist. Even from where I'd stopped behind the torch-darkened shapes of Snude and Serafina, I could see the golden glitter of the rutilated quartz.

You might think at such a time I'd have no thought for anything else. But it was just then as Serafina turned, profile edged by refracted light, her glance held fast as it locked with mine, that it came over me like a bolt from the sky I didn't want this girl to pass out of my life. It was a startling revelation whose impact shook me clean to my boots. Having no idea how to cope with it or the look I read in those dark, widened eyes, almost frightened by such an alarming discovery, I wrenched my glance away from hers.

I heard her gasp in a choked kind of whisper, "Do you suppose this is some of the Peralta ore?"

Trying to pull myself together with Snude's sharp stare fastening onto my face, I said with conviction, "It just about has to be. I think we're standing in their Number Four Mine, the only one not shown on your map. And very possibly, I reckon, the best of the lot."

Chapter Ten

A RUDE AWAKENING

"Going to be quite a task," Snude said, looking around, "getting all this ore packed back to our camp."

I reckoned it plain from the way he spoke it was a chore he regarded with no little satisfaction.

Serafina, wheeling to look at him, said, "Rather late in the day to begin that now, isn't it?"

"Oh, we can't do it today. I was thinking some of us will have to stay in camp when we're bringing it down. No chance of moving it all at one swoop."

"Right on target," I nodded. "Handling this stuff won't be any cinch. Getting it from here to your bank in Tucson is likely to give us plenty of headaches. Without more men I can't see how you'll do it. And there's other knotty problems."

Snude with a tolerant twist of the lips said, "What do you feel will be the knottiest problems?"

"Where'll you get your men? While you're gettin' them, who'll watch out for what we've got here now that we've opened up a way to get at it? And who'll watch out for it while it's being moved? Finding reliable men is likely to be hard enough. Finding competent ones that are also reliable will be a heap like scratchin' your ear with your elbow. After you've got all that in hand, and brought in more mules and got them packed, you'll have to get this stuff across a heap of rough country which, by that time, is likely to be crawlin' with cutthroats and outlaws of every description."

While this was being digested, I said, "On top of that you've got this girl to watch out for."

This got me a grateful look from Serafina, though she said with her chin up, "I can look out for myself."

Snude said then in his arbitrary fashion, "I expect the county sheriff can be talked into providing all the men we'll need once he understands the nature of this operation."

And, despite Spartokori's fish-eyed look, that was where my misgivings were left.

By the time we had all got out of the tunnel and rid ourselves of its musty air, and Snude was setting off in the lead for our horses, I'd a full-blown hunch that trouble and this outfit were not far apart. This foreboding took on a new dimension when I noticed the way Spartokori, every few steps, was twisting his head for a look toward our camp site.

Waiting for me to come up with him, he said, "Stranger down there chinnin' with Schroeder." While I was trying to pick them out of the lengthening shadows he added, "Over by our tarp-covered mound of supplies."

He was absolutely right. "You've got sharp eyes." Though unable at this distance to make out the man's features, he was obviously someone I hadn't seen before, a tall, lanky critter in cowpuncher garb, and it looked like to me they were having quite a chat. Neither Cookson nor Quintada was anywhere in sight.

Reaching our horses, I found that Snude evidently had made the same discovery. The look on that highboned face was far from pleasant. Without any gab he started for camp the moment his butt settled into the saddle.

Whatever thoughts the sight had put in his noggin, he was not so wrapped up in them as to disregard the hazards of the terrain. He kept his horse at a walk, the rest of us likewise. Spartokori too, though obviously bothered, kept his notions to himself.

Arriving at camp about an hour later, we found a fire cheerfully burning with them all sitting round it, looking as comfortable as four peas in the same pod. Snude gruffly ordered Quintada to take care of our horses and, dismounting, strode straight over to confront the fellow. Without any pretense of surprise or friendly interest, he said coldly, "What are you doing here, Flake?"

"Didn't expect you'd remember me after the brush-off I got from you at the bank," the man said, thinly smiling. "Just happened to see your fire as I was passing and thought I'd drop by and see how you were doing. Understand you've found a mine."

This Flake looked to be somewhere in his middle sixties, about the same age as Snude, but more compact despite his appearance of having been drawn through a knot hole. He had a cold-jawed face and a mean pair of eyes that revealed no sign of being bothered in the least by Snude's belligerent attitude.

"What I may or may not have found is no concern of yours, Ben Flake."

"Well, there's gratitude for you. Don't you reckon it's about time you and me had a powwow?"

"I've said all I had to say when you came sucking around for a loan."

Flake's stare moved over him like a grit-filled wind off the desert. Then he said with a bark of a laugh, "Same old Snude. Same tight-ass bastard who beat me down to half its worth for that ore my old man dug up at the Massacre Grounds. Only this time," he said in a raspy voice, "you'll not get away with it."

Snude with a jerk of his chin at Schroeder went off toward our mound of supplies where he wheeled to wait for Schroeder to come up with him. But Schroeder hadn't moved; he was still hunkered down where he'd been when Snude left. Even from where I stood with Serafina and the Greek, I could see the black hate boiling out of Snude's stare.

The Circle Dot owner looked at Schroeder with a laugh. "He'll have his knife out for you, Butch. Better keep your eyes skinned."

Schroeder's tight-lipped expression remained as enigmatic as ever. Not even by so much as a shrug of the shoulders could you find any clue to what was going on back of those slate-colored eyes.

Flake, glancing around, said, "When do you fellers generally put on the nosebags?"

Cookson, seeming to come out of a trance, said he'd get right at it and went over to dig his cooking utensils from under the tarp.

I steered Serafina away from the fire and over toward the rock where our bedrolls were piled. "Could be a good idea for you to go to your tent and get a little rest while Bob's hasslin' with his pots," I suggested.

After searching my face with a pretty sharp look, she took my advice and I went back to where Spartokori had squatted. "No love lost between this pelican and Snude it looks like," he muttered. "Don't seem like the sort I'd care to get chummy with."

Having said this he shoved up and moved off.

I hadn't seen any sense in mentioning to the Greek that Snude had wanted to stop by Flake's place on the way up here, but I did turn it over once or twice in my head while waiting for Bob to get our vittles off the fire. About all Bob appeared able to fix was boiled beans, fried beans, and refried beans. This time it was boiled beans and a panful of his hard-as-rock biscuits.

"I've ate better," Flake remarked, tossing his utensils into the wreck pan after belching.

Cookson scowled but kept his thoughts to himself. I was certainly expecting, having outstayed his welcome, Flake would get on his horse and head for whatever had fetched him out here, but he showed no signs of leaving. It was full dark now and I wondered if he was fixing to bed down here with the rest of us, wanted or not. The troubled thoughts that had hold of me ever since crawling into that mine tunnel took a darker, more worrisome clutch as I watched him pull the rolled blankets off the back of his mouse-colored horse and, moments later, take the saddle off too.

Across the fire I noticed Spartokori blackly frowning at the gall of this performance, and Cookson watching with no hint of the amusement so frequently prevalent while regarding the antics of those around him. By all the signs and signal smokes violence was due to erupt any moment.

Schroeder allowed he was going to turn in and got up and went off to pick up his bedding. I couldn't see Snude, but Spartokori, with a last black look in Flake's direction, also took himself off. I supposed Quintada had found himself a nest. Not caring to be left with this encroaching bastard, I got onto my feet with a pretended yawn and quit the fire to find my own cover off a few paces behind the dim outlines of Serafina's tent. Still, in the grip of my disturbed notions, it took me a good while to get to sleep but, listening to the crickets, I must have finally dozed off.

It seemed like I'd scarcely got my eyes closed when a jabber of voices jerked me awake to find Cookson's shocked face in the cold light of dawn scarcely six inches from my own.

"What the hell?" I growled, getting onto an elbow, peering up at him blearily as he stepped back away from me.

"Wake up," he muttered. "Somebody's killed that son of a bitch!"

I guess my wits weren't working as well as they might have

86

been. Only fellow in my head rightly fitting that description was our domineering banker.

"Snude?" I said.

"No . . . that god-damned Flake." He rasped a hand across his whiskers. "Quintada just found him with a knife buried back of his wishbone. You reckon Snude did it?"

"He was riled enough, I expect. Hard to picture Snude with a knife, though."

Bob shook his head. "That lanky sidewinder looked like trouble first time I laid eyes on him."

"When was that?" I said, getting onto my feet.

His face came around to peer at me again. I thought I could read a startled speculation somewhere back in the depths of that stare. "When the bugger showed up yesterday and got off his horse like he expected we was going to roll out the red carpet."

"What did Schroeder have to say? He act like they were acquainted?"

He looked to be pushing that around in his head. "Not that I noticed. Butch was his usual sour-faced self. Never opened his mouth while I was around. I went off after a spell and had me a nap. When I came back, Quintada was off some place. Taking care of the mules, I reckon."

"So them two had the place to themselves for a while."

"Well, yes, I suppose they did. Any reason they shouldn't have?"

"On the way down we saw the pair of them over where we stacked the supplies. Seemed to be having quite a conversation."

Bob scratched his head. "No law against it. Oh!" he said with narrowed stare, "you figure those two were setting up something?"

"Well, it wouldn't surprise me. Where is Flake now . . . what's left of him?"

"Snude said we better plant him, so that's what we did."

I pushed a hand along my jaw. "Didn't you think that was hurrying it a mite?"

"Said he didn't want no damn' buzzards circling overhead. . . ."

"Probably right about that. We're not in a good position to be invitin' attention with that ore on our hands."

Nodding, Bob added, "Figured he was mostly concerned about the girl. Didn't want her getting upset, he said. With Flake out of sight, if she thought about the bugger at all, she'd think he'd simply gone off about his business."

"Yes, well I expect any business he had was right here. No saddle tramp snuck into this camp to finish him off, if that's what you're thinkin'. Somebody right here took care of that rascal. One of us," I said grimly. "And, much as I'd like to, I don't think it was Snude."

"But that's crazy," Bob spluttered. "None of us knew him. . . !"

"Snude knew him. I'd guess Schroeder did, too. When you're looking to cook up some devilment, you don't go around propositioning strangers. Try using your noodle, Bob! Quintada may have known him. So might Spartokori. They've probably both got connections with people you wouldn't invite home to dinner."

Bob's glance juned around. "I suppose you're right."

"What about Bluff Spring Mountain? You going to tell him or shall I?"

He stood a while, staring, rummaging my face. "Time to have told him was back on that mountain. You go opening your mouth now. . . ."

"I wouldn't have to mention you."

"This is a hell of a time to bring something like that up. You want to cut yourself out of this whole deal?" He said, direfully urgent: "You want to wind up like Flake?"

I hadn't thought about that. I could see, with tempers being what they were right now, what he said was a distinct possibility.

He took hold of my arm. "That whole cache ain't worth such

a risk. If you got to be squeamish, just tip off Spartokori to the pots you found up there. That'll get you off the hook." Then he said, still eyeing me, "If you want, I'll put a bug in his ear."

He went off, past the tent, toward where Quintada was building up the fire, leaving me tangled in my own bitter thoughts.

After a breakfast of fried boiled beans and johnnycake with damn' little talk and no mention of Flake, no sign of his blankets or that mouse-colored horse, Snude gruffly announced that Quintada, Cookson, and Schroeder would be going up to the mine with him. He told Quintada to bring up their horses.

"The rest of you," he said, "will be staying here in camp, taking care of the animals, and keeping your eyes peeled."

Ten minutes later they loped off toward the mountain.

The Greek observed, "Right sociable this morning. Just one big happy family," and busied himself rolling up a smoke.

Serafina said, "I'm getting a little tired of *frijoles*. Let's go see if we can scare up some rabbits."

So I picked up my Winchester and we set off toward the brush. Soon as we got out of earshot, I said: "Where's your gun?"

She looked a little surprised. "A double-action Colt isn't much good for shooting rabbits."

"Never mind that. Hereafter you keep it with you. Don't come out of your tent unarmed."

Her astonishment was plain. "What's got into you fellows this morning? Gulping your breakfast with scarcely a word. Watching each other like a bunch of strange dogs. Somebody tell you the sky was about to fall?"

"It could happen. I don't like to worry you, but there's a killer loose in this outfit. I think you should know it. That feller, Flake, got rubbed out last night. Somebody shoved a knife in his back. Snude made them bury him before you got up."

Her cheeks turned pale. Her eyes looked enormous. When she found her voice, the only thing she asked was: "Who do you think killed him?"

"I don't think it was Snude. Too obvious and, if Snude wanted to be rid of him, I don't think he'd use a knife. It may or may not be concerned with what we found up there yesterday, but until we get away from this mountain you better be on your guard every minute. I wish the hell you were out of this."

She gave my arm a squeeze with her fingers. "We better start looking for rabbits," she said.

I finally bagged three, and we went back to camp where I took care of them. She told Spartokori, "We'll have them for supper."

After munching some jerky and emptying a can of tomatoes apiece, Serafina went into her tent. The Greek gave me a look, and we moved off to where our supplies were stacked. He cleared his throat angrily and zeroed in on a passing tumblebug. "What does it look like to you?"

"Same as it does to you, I expect. Feller acted like he was aiming to move in and somebody here didn't like it, I'd say."

"Kind of drastic way of getting shut of the bugger."

"Guess you heard what he said, same as the rest of us. Be interestin' to know who tipped him off. We can be sure of one thing. It wasn't the jasper who left the knife in him."

I knew the Greek for a dealer in Indian artifacts and other collectibles and probably anything else that would show a profit. He was a cautious poker player. He held a license to import and export. In our once-a-month acquaintance this was all I'd discovered.

"Kind of thing to put a man on edge."

I nodded. "Not a comfortable thing to live with certainly."

Spartokori snorted. "Don't like the idea of chewin' my vittles alongside a back-stabbing murderer."

"Guess we'll just have to keep our eyes skinned."

The Greek squirmed around in his clothes and pulled at his

lip, eyeing me obliquely. "Just whereabouts is that cave you and Cookson got into? Old pots, he said. You find anything else?"

"Handful of emeralds and some old Spanish coins."

He peered at me sharply. "How come you didn't fetch 'em down?"

I showed him a grin. "Not enough to go around and too much for one haul."

"Yeah," he said dryly, "I can understand that."

"You're welcome to them if you want to go to the bother."

It was his turn to grin. "I ain't leaving this mountain till the rest of you do."

Serafina's stew was bubbling merrily in the pot when Snude and the other three came down from the mine. Snude, smiling at her, said, "Was afraid we'd be treated to more beans and hardtack."

Cookson sauntered up to the fire in time to catch that and said with sore feeling, "If you can find another cook, he can have my apron anytime."

Quintada went off with their horses. "Don't be too long," Serafina called after him. "Soon as the biscuits are done, we'll be eating."

"What did you think of our find?" Spartokori asked Schroeder.

"Looks a pretty good haul if we can get back to town with it."

"Yeah," Bob said. "That could take some doing."

Serafina said, "We're going to need more men and pack animals Chuck thinks."

"It isn't going to be easy to find competent help. Mister Snude," I mentioned, slanching a look at him, "is of the opinion he can talk the sheriff into coming up with them."

Schroeder grunted. "Why don't we have Quintada fetch in some of his smuggler friends? They'll make short work of it."

Chapter Eleven

BLOOD ON THE MOON

"And of us, too, probably," Bob said sourly.

Snude looked like he was giving it real thought. "You know," he said suddenly, "that just might work out to everyone's advantage. Cheaper, too. Cheaper and quicker. No lallygagging around with them on the job."

"Who'll ride herd on them?" Spartokori inquired. "Somebody'd have to, or we'd find ourselves holding the short end of the stick."

Cookson said, looking around at Snude, "You can't be serious!"

The banker said, "I don't see why not. It'll be giving them some honest work for a change. Who knows the trails any better than they do? They'd be up to every dodge in the book. And with that bunch around who'd try to stop us?"

I couldn't help feeling he meant every word. I even wondered if maybe it wasn't so crazy, after all. You fight fire with fire. Snude certainly understood the risks we'd be running by packing all that gold across those empty miles. Like he said, that bunch would know all the dodges. They were used to taking chances and would, as he said, be a pretty convincing deterrent to brush runners, drifters, and plain downright uglies. Regardless, if the banker made up his mind to go this route, I didn't see how he could be talked out of it.

With the pots, the pans, and the eating tools well scrubbed by sand and elbow grease, Serafina now rejoined the confab around the fire. It must have been eight-thirty or nine when I finally rose to my feet. It had been a long day and, after last night's happening, this jawing I figured could go on for hours. Nobody was anxious to be seeking his blankets with the dread possibility of sharing Flake's fate.

I left them still wrangling and went off with my soogans to find me a place where the moon couldn't shine, fetching along my rifle, ostensibly to keep it away from the dew but really to make sure it didn't get tampered with. Trust, in this camp, was becoming scarcer than hen's teeth.

I went clean to the outer edge of things, a couple dozen feet beyond the tent but where I could still keep one eye cocked on it, before finding a covert that suited me. I scraped a place for my hips, took the rifle under the cover, and prepared to endure another chancy night, fairly certain the disturbing thoughts I went to bed with would keep me unwanted company. They did.

I couldn't help recalling the tales I'd heard about folks who had never come out of these mountains, and there had been plenty of them. Now there was Flake who had been cut short before playing out his hand. The bugger had obviously had something on Snude, perhaps something out of the banker's past. Whatever, it must have been something pretty obnoxious for Flake to think it would fetch him a place in our outfit.

I got to wondering again which of my companions had thrust that knife in him. Spartokori packed a knife. I had seen it. Quintada had a Bowie knife. Cookson didn't, but as cook for this bunch there'd be sharp blades available. Schroeder, I thought, would have used a gun, and I wondered again if he had gunned down my mother back in Texas that night. I could still see that *hombre*, but age would have changed him as it undoubtedly had Schroeder.

Two things I felt pretty sure of — that this was the abandoned

93

Number Four Mine the Peraltas had quit in their panicked flight from the Apaches who had killed them, and that here was the source of Jake Walzer's gold. Up there yesterday in the depths of that tunnel, I'd felt distinctly uneasy. There'd been an eerie feeling coming out of that passage all those tons of piled-up rock hanging over our heads could not reasonably account for — something dangerous and evil. Was it the vestiges of left-over fright from those long-gone Peraltas or something more immediate, some emanation from the minds or thoughts of Snude or Spartokori? Or had it come from the very mountain itself, anchored here among its shattered rocks in sun-baked isolation, brooding through the quiet of centuries, gathering itself, yearning to give voice to the anguish in its hidden depths?

Nothing untoward appeared to have got itself afoot while the night's spooky shadows moved across my nervous vigil. The new day came with a lifting breeze as Bob moved past in his hunt for wood to build up the fire. I threw back my covers and got up and stretched, looking to see who else was stirring.

Bob came back with an armload of brush. "Trust you're feeling more chipper than I am. You honestly think he's serious about that?"

"If you mean asking those smugglers into this deal, the answer is yes. What's more, I think they'll jump at the chance when Quintada tells them what we've got hold of."

I saw Schroeder, off a piece, rolling up his blanket. They were all up, it looked like, except Serafina and Quintada. I said, "I don't see Quintada."

"Gone after them, I reckon," Bob grunted, moving off with his greasewood stems in the direction of the ashes left from last night's fire.

"Who's tendin' the mules?" I called after him.

He said sourly, "Who do you suppose . . . me, of course!"

As I rounded the tent, Serafina emerged in boots and jeans

and a yellow print shirt with cornflowers on it. *"Buenos días,"* she murmured, with something less than her usual bright smile. Still, she was bearing up a heap better than one might expect of a city girl not yet out of her teens. I doffed my hat, sketched her a nod of approval.

"When," I said, "did your uncle die?"

"Gonzales?" She thought a few moments. "Several years ago. I'm not sure of the date. It was less than a week after giving me the map. I didn't live with him, though sometimes . . . infrequently . . . he would come to see me for an hour or two. It was on one of those visits that he left a manila envelope with me and said he wanted me to have it. The map was inside. Several days later I was told by José Quintada that my uncle had been thrown from a horse."

"What do you suppose he was doing on a horse, a man in his eighties who walked with a cane?"

Her look jumped at me, startled. "I hadn't thought of that . . . I don't believe he'd been on a horse in years."

"He lived, I think you told me, with José Quintada?"

"Yes. Do you suppose . . . Pepe claims they're no relation, but . . . ?"

"It's a common enough name. But I think it's something that would bear looking into since you were told he died in so unlikely a manner."

"Do you think there might be a connection between our Quintada and that man Flake?"

"It . . . I don't know. A bit of thought on the subject can't do much harm. Didn't you say Gonzales was the only one to survive that massacre when the Peralta brothers were killed with their peons over near Goldfield?"

"Yes. Luckily he wasn't with them. He once told me he knew nothing about it until several days after it happened. He never went into the Superstitions again. Some of the fondest memories

95

of myself as a little girl are connected with my uncle."

"The things I remember with the most satisfaction are my years as a cowhand on the tumble-down ranch just beyond the far side of this mountain."

She said, wrinkling her nose, "I have to go . . . I promised Bob last night I'd fix breakfast this morning. . . ."

"Good!" I grinned. "Even the Mexican half of me is beginnin' to rebel at the prospect of confronting another batch of *frijoles*."

Her brows shot up. "A wetback . . . you? With a name like Brannigan?"

"You haven't noticed my flair for puttin' off till tomorrow chores most gringos would've done yesterday?"

Still chuckling, she hurried off toward the fire. I watched her go with lifting spirits, that laugh exorcising some part of the guilt that was gnawing at me for not having shared with this outfit the find we'd uncovered above Bluff Spring. It was getting hard to keep my mind off this girl. Flake, the way I saw him now, must have been some way involved in Gonzales's death. Why had Snude been so anxious to chin with him just before we'd got into these mountains and been so hostile when the fellow'd come riding into our camp — unless the pair of them knew more than was healthy about the death of Serafina's uncle? And where did Quintada fit into that business?

There were plenty of questions with no firm answers. Somewhere I seemed to have heard or read that one of those old Peralta mines had been discovered by Gonzales. Had it been Number Four?

Snude came striding up just then. "I sent off Quintada to round up his smugglers. There's not much we can do before he gets back with them and that's likely to take the best part of a week. I'm going to put two of you up there as guards. Soon as we eat, you'll go up there with Schroeder. That way you can keep an eye on each other."

I nodded. "If anyone else comes nosing around . . . ?"

"Shoot first and gab later," he said through a scowl, and strode off toward the fire.

I shouldered my blankets, went over to where our supplies were stacked, and dropped them alongside. Seeing Cookson headed for the creek with the mules, I reckoned he'd not be joining us for breakfast since most of us can't do but one thing at a time.

Having griddle cakes for a change was a real treat for me. Though I wasn't pleased by the prospect of spending all day on that mountain with the taciturn Schroeder, I was nonetheless glad that it wouldn't be in the dark I'd have to do this. Try as I would, I couldn't like the fellow and trusted him no farther than I could have flung a bobcat. Finished with eating, we saddled up and took off.

It looked to be another hot day, but at least on the mountain one could hope for an occasional breeze. Now that we'd found a better way of getting up there, it didn't take as long as it had that first time when I'd gone up with Serafina, Snude, and the Greek. Nor did we have nearly as much walking to do after getting out of our saddles.

"Wonder what's on top," Schroeder mused, looking round at me.

"Can't say. Never been up there."

"Mebbe we ought to find out," he suggested.

"What in the world for?"

"In a situation like this I like to know where I'm at."

"Well, you can look if you want. I've had enough climbing already to suit me."

By the time we got to the ledge that half hid the cave, I dropped on my butt to drag in some fresh air while considering the great sweep of country spread out down below. I had my lever-action Winchester comfortably resting across my lap and was pleased we'd left our mounts within easy range. One thing I was not particularly anxious to experience was being left afoot in this chunk of desolation.

"Where you reckon them two no-accounts have got to?" Schroeder asked, sort of casually as he stood peering about.

"I'll give odds they're not far off."

"What do you think of Snude sendin' for them smugglers?"

"I don't think much of it. Tell you the truth, it kind of gives me the shivers."

"Don't show," he observed, like he had been studying me. "What part of Texas do you hail from, if you don't mind my askin'?"

"I don't mind," I said.

In the lengthening quiet I could feel his fish-eyed stare. With the rifle laying there ready in my lap and a finger not three inches from the trigger, I didn't have to watch the bugger. My ears would detect any hostile move.

With a grunt he said, "I'm goin' up for a look."

"Sure," I said, still eyeing the view.

After he'd got up out of earshot, another stretch of wondering grabbed me. More and more this poker-faced varmint was beginning to fit into the picture stamped in my head of that expressionless bastard crouched above a smoking gun by the steps to the claim shack back in Texas the night my mother was cut off in her prime. An ugly thought, and there was no comfort in me as the two sides of my nature struggled for control. I was often mixed up in my own mind and I guess to most folks I was a difficult person. I expect it's what came of being a mixed breed, each of the warring notions inside me evolved from a heritage only barely compatible, the gringo half urging caution if not tolerance, the darker side of me frequently reckless and often uncaring in the grip of strong feelings. The kind that had hold of me thinking of Schroeder.

It was, I figured, a pretty safe bet that him and Snude were tied into this together, Snude the conniver and Schroeder his hatchet man. Thinking back on this deal, it seemed to me that from the start Snude's only interest had been to get to this mountain. It appeared pretty likely he must have been driven by something he'd learned from that hardcase, Ben Flake, the one I'd been told had been Silverlock in the days of Jake Walzer.

I swore under my breath. It looked plain enough now why Snude had wanted us with him — myself he'd relied on to find him this mountain. What he'd found up there was no job for one man. Not even the seven of us were enough to get that ore out of there and over those miles between here and his bank. Hence the need for Quintada and his smuggling connections. How Snude aimed to control them I sure couldn't figure; he wasn't the sort needlessly to part with a penny. Quintada's mention of this treasure would fetch them all right — but how could we keep them from making off with it? By and large these swashbuckling bandits had to be pretty desperate men.

All this thinking was making my head ache, but something else was also on my mind — that pair of footloose drifters. And how much reliance, I thought with a curse, could you place in Bob Cookson? Or Spartokori? The more I considered what I'd got myself into, the less I liked it.

The smartest thing I could do was cut my losses, latch onto Serafina, and get the hell out of here. It was plain as paint what I ought to do. Doing it, however, was something else. Ever turn your back on a fortune? I'd taken chips in the go-around and it just wasn't in me to throw in my hand.

Scarcely had I reached this idiot's conclusion than I thought I heard a yell. Fixing my sights for the top of the mountain, I discovered it was Schroeder trying to get my attention. Hands cupped about his mouth, he shouted, "Get your ass up here . . . somethin' I want you to see!"

Though it occurred to me this could well be a ruse to put me where I could be thrown off the mountain, I wasn't about to let no potbellied gringo tell the rest of the outfit I'd been scared to go up there. While I was almost convinced he was the bugger I thought he was, I didn't think he could be that sure of me, or I'd have been taken care of already.

It was rugged work, and I had no mind to break a leg getting up there. Once I'd got past the boulder-blocked entrance to the tunnel, the climb still ahead appeared even more hazardous and, with every inch of me alert, I took my time to do it. Whatever he wanted could wait till I got there. Those last ten feet looked hair-raisingly precarious. Eventually I got over the last crumbly ledge and, breathing hard, stood up to find him fixedly staring at a crack in the bald rock. It was probably six inches wide and seemed to go clean across the caprock.

"What about it?" I said. "I've seen plenty of cracked rock in this mountain. If that's all you've got me up here to look at. . . ."

"Put your fist in it."

Watching out for some trick, I got down on one knee and in that position caught the smell coming out of it. It stunk like a seven-day cadaver.

"Put your fist in it." Schroeder growled.

Staring up at him, ready to duck, I gingerly lowered my left hand into the mouth of the crack and felt the hot air pulsing up my arm like there was a fire down there some place. I got onto my feet. We were eyeing each other, my suspicions discarded as I thought about this and gulped in some fresh air.

He said, "What do you think?"

What I thought made no sense.

Schroeder said, "One time in the islands I smelt somethin' like that."

We eyed each other some more, both of us scowling at things

100

you couldn't see.

He said, "You reckon I better go down and tell Snude?"

I nodded. I wasn't thinking any more about possible intruders. "We'll both go," I told him.

When we informed Snude, he said, "What the hell are you talking about?"

He looked like the both of us had gone off our rockers.

"You can laugh if you want," Schroeder said grimly, "but I'm tellin' you that mountain's likely to blow itself up!"

"Of all the crack-brained . . . !"

"I think he's right," I butted in to say. "Go up there and take a sniff for yourself, feel the heat that's coming up out of that crack. I think that mountain is restin' right now on top of a volcano."

"Keep your voice down, you fool!" Snude glared at me furiously. "You want to throw this whole damned camp in a uproar? That's the craziest yarn I've heard in a coon's age!"

"You'll change your mind if you go up there," Schroeder muttered.

"I don't need to go anywhere to know you fools must have got into rattleweed. A volcano!" he snorted. "There hasn't been anything like that around here in years. Now get back up there and keep. . . ."

"Not me," Schroeder said. "I know when I'm well off."

It looked to me like the banker was about to bust his surcingle.

"Spartokori!" he yelled. "Cookson . . . get over here!" When they came up to us, he growled: "Get up on that mountain and keep a watch for those saddle tramps."

We'd got off our mounts but still had hold of the reins.

"Here . . . where you going?" Snude demanded as the pair turned away.

Bob said, "Ain't expecting us to walk, are you?"

"What's the matter with these two? They're already saddled."

"You're not takin' my horse on that mountain," Schroeder said, looking ugly.

Spartokori, puzzled, looked from Schroeder to Snude.

Cookson said, "I prefer my own," and went off to pick up his rope before heading toward the cavvy.

Spartokori, staring at Schroeder, said, "You run into a batch of snakes up there?"

"No snakes," I said. "Take mine if you want."

He peered at Snude again, took the reins I held out, and climbed into the saddle, looking as though he was half minded not to. "Thought you boys was stayin' up there till supper."

"We came down to report," I said, "and the boss didn't like it."

The Greek was no fool and looked a long way from satisfied. But when Bob came up, Spartokori rode off with him.

"Volcanoes!" Snude said, disgusted. "What you smelled was some animal fell in there and couldn't get out. Anytime you got a volcano, you got smoke coming out of it. You see any smoke?"

Schroeder, grimacing, shook his head.

"There you are then," Snude declared in his know-it-all fashion. "No smoke, no volcano," and, like that settled it, walked off and left us.

Schroeder plainly didn't believe. I was not sure I believed this, either.

"He's due for a hemorrhage," Schroeder growled, "when it's too late to get that damned ore outa there." He sent a black scowl after Snude and spat. "I've got a good mind to get mine out right now!"

It looked like a good time to find out something. I said, "You might get it out, but I doubt you'll keep it."

I might as well have gone fishing with an empty hook for all the change that jarred out of Schroeder. It never even dredged up his bullypuss grin. He towed his horse toward the rest of our livestock without opening the slit he used for a mouth.

Serafina said, as I stood staring after him, "What's up, Chuck?"

I shrugged. "Hard telling. Don't know if that gazebo is lined up with Snude or workin' this solo." I saw no point in getting her wind up. "You know, dadburn I'm pretty fond of you, Serafina."

All I got out of that was a quick look of amusement. "That's the Brannigan half of you adding up shares," she grinned.

"And here I figured sweet talk was the language of courtship," I said, real solemnly. "Guess it don't pay to count chickens till you've got 'em in the coop. How would you feel if there weren't any shares?"

"Are you trying to tell me something?"

"Just wonderin', is all."

"I'll leave you at it, then. With Bob off on the mountain I'd better go see what can be rounded up for supper."

Looking after her, I seemed finally to have got it straight in my head what I wanted from the future. Never having had a heap to jingle in my pockets, I reminded myself that money, though mighty handy, was no guarantee of happiness. That I could dredge up such a thought considerably astonished me.

While I was standing there turning it over, Snude came back to say: "Better make yourself useful and start feeding those mules."

Chapter Twelve

FLAMES ABOVE THE MOUNTAIN

Spartokori and Bob came down during the shank of the afternoon to make sure their names were in the pot for some of Serafina's supper of corned beef, baked potatoes, and another sampling of her top-notch biscuits. All of us could see this didn't set well with our demanding boss.

"Who," he wanted to be told, "is looking out for our property?"

"Couple eagles up there keeping an eye on it," Bob said. "I don't know what you're frettin' about. If those two vagrants come messing around, we can see them from here."

That got him the kind of look no red-blooded *hombre* would stomach unless it came from his wife. Bob just grinned and the Greek had the gall to ask, "When are you taking a turn up there, Snude?"

The banker flung around to growl at me, "I want you up there soon as you finish eating, Brannigan."

"Let's get this straight, once and for all," I growled back at him. "The only peon in this outfit is Pepe Quintada. Since you've sent him off to fetch in those gun-runnin' friends of his, I reckon you'll just have to wait till he gets back. I don't mind takin' a turn feeding mules, but that's as far as it goes."

I suppose this was tantamount to open rebellion but, in the feisty mood I had worked myself into, I was ready to let the chips fall where they would. He probably saw that. In any event, he grabbed up a pan and some eating tools and made for the pot where the tinned beef was simmering. So nobody that night went up to stand guard.

I thought a guard was better needed to keep an eye on the supplies and livestock. They represented the best means we had of getting out of there if something came up we weren't able to handle. Not caring to push myself into Snude's category, I hobbled my lip and went off to spread my bed in easy reach of my horse and was still pondering that discovery Schroeder had made when sleep overtook me.

It wasn't much past dawn when a babble of excited voices woke me. I shoved up on my elbow to find the whole bunch staring up at the mountain. It didn't take me long to see the cause of the uproar. I had no doubt it was smoke we were looking at. Wind was chasing it off the crown in a ragged cloud, and I got myself afoot in a hurry.

Heading for the squabble, I heard Snude's angry shout and Schroeder's bull voice tearing right through it. As I came up to them, he was yelling, "Breakfast hell! If we're to save any of that ore, we better get up there straightaway and start luggin' it out. Right now that lava's still under the mountain, but how long it'll stay there is anybody's guess! Once it starts up, it's likely to take the whole inside of that rock pile right along with it!"

Spartokori said, "He's right about that . . . I've seen it happen. It could do that for months without bustin' loose. But once she goes that ore's going with it!"

"Won't do much good," I said, "stackin' it outside. Anything we save'll have to be taken clean away and, if it really lets go, we could lose what's here, too. If one of you'll give me a hand, I'll get the mules ready. It'll have to come off the mountain by mule pack if we're to save any amount of it."

And then, just when it seemed this potential disaster might have united us in a common needful effort, who should come

riding into our camp but Barry Storm whose likeness was a familiar sight in the Phoenix and Tucson papers as the foremost
authority on the Lost Dutchman and this entire rock-ribbed area.
All the talk fell away, throats drying up like a last year's leaf
as our outfit took in his presence. Consternation could not have
been more apparent had a full-blown plague stumbled into our
midst.

Looking us over with a chuckle, Storm said, "You make me
feel about as welcome as a skunk at a church picnic. What's
the matter with you guys? Do I look like I'm contagious?"

Bob said, scowling, "It's that god-damned mountain! You see
the smoke coming out of it? You reckon that bugger's going
to blow wide open?"

"Can't see no need for getting into a sweat. That peak's been
lettin' off steam for years, and it hasn't blown yet. Every once
in a while she sends up a puff or two. No cause for alarm."

"What I've been trying to tell these yahoos," Snude proclaimed.
"How's things with you, Barry?"

"Still lookin'," Storm said.

"Don't need any help, do you?" Cookson asked as though ready
to offer his services.

This fellow, I thought, looked just like his pictures, big-nosed,
mustached, a corrugation of wrinkles fanning out from the
twinkling eyes beneath his cuffed-back hat, shirt pockets stuffed
with notebooks and pencils.

"No," he said, sharing his grin with all of us. "I like to play
a lone hand. You boys havin' any luck?"

Spartokori said, "Sure. We been trying to figure how to cut
up a bonanza."

"Usual cause of trouble when you take in partners."

Serafina came up from the direction of our fire. "We're just
about to eat," she smiled. "Better sit in and pad your stomach.
If you don't mind taking pot luck."

"Obliged," Storm said. "T'ain't much I like better than eat-in'."

After putting that breakfast away, we sat around fidgeting like a panful of eels while Storm, as if he had all the time in the world, told us about the Lost Dutchman he'd been hunting for years. A big name in the treasure-hunting fraternity, he had a fund of interesting anecdotes, well laced with colorful characters.

"Old Gonzales," he said, "was the smart one, strikin' off for himself, not content to string along with the rest. Told me once, just before he kicked off, he'd found their Number Four Mine and barely got out ahead of the Apaches."

I noticed Snude prick up his ears. "Don't suppose he mentioned whereabouts this was?"

"Canny old rooster," Storm chuckled. "I've always figured he might've told one of his nephews, but no Peralta's been prowlin' these mountains in my time. Lots of stories about 'em. I tried to run down a few but didn't get any place. Lots of fellers claim-in' to have maps but those I bumped into all wanted to sell 'em." He chuckled again. "Been considerable change around an' about since that last quake. Whole sections altered. Pretty hard now to recognize some of these slopes."

Schroeder said, "You musta been powerful young at the time."

"I wasn't around," Storm said with a grin. "Just stands to reason. Even a good map would be pretty useless. All this country was under water once . . . big inland sea. I've found petrified clam shells, clams still in 'em, on some of these mountains. Even run onto bones of dinosaurs and mammoths. Lot of marshes through here in those days."

"You think these mountains were under water?" Snude looked incredulous.

"Plates, shifting somewhere, make a chain reaction. You go that far back," Storm pointed out, "there weren't any mountains where we're at right now. They were just thrown up out of

107

the sea bed, I reckon."

"You mentioned quakes," I said, "and that a lot of this country was altered by them. To the best of my knowledge . . . which's not a great deal . . . the Peraltas weren't here until late in the 'thirties."

Storm nodded. "That's about right."

The man was a bundle of information, some of it fact and, I reckoned, a heap of it fancy. It got so I wasn't half listening, taken up right then with notions of my own. Whether the mountain blew or didn't blow, the threat was there looming large in our minds. Time, suddenly important, was the big factor now that the fellow was wasting so much of it. We still had to get in there to bring out the ore. Dangerous or not, nobody wanted to let go of it.

I wanted my share as much as anyone, and more if I could get it. Being downright frank, I was badly in need of a stake and wasn't getting any younger. I wanted Serafina, but not with her getting two shares to my one. What I was trying to shape in my head was how I could come out of this as well off, financially speaking, as she would be if we got this ore to market.

It had occurred to me, if handled right, this might be possible. I thought I could see how to go about it, how I might get them to agree I should have a bigger share. This required stretching out Storm's visit to let the threat of that mountain become as overwhelming as possible in the minds of my partners. There was a real danger there and every minute we dawdled before getting at it was going to magnify the risk. We all had to be gamblers to have entered into this damned venture and, if the risk could be made to seem intolerable enough, I thought I could swing it.

Keeping our unwelcome visitor here with that smoke hanging over us, half covering the sky and almost blotting out the sun, would be eventually turning them frantic and all the more so since, without arousing his suspicions, they were powerless to be rid of Storm. If I could hold him here long enough, there wasn't one of them would dare go into that tunnel, gold or no gold.

I could see the growing fright in Spartokori's face every time his glance furtively lifted to scan the awful pall hanging over us. Like Schroeder had claimed, he may have seen a mountain blast off in the islands, but I was heavily banking on what Storm had told us about smoke pouring out of Tortilla before.

It was already past noon and I thought, if he could be kept a mite longer, Serafina would feel obligated to invite him to share another meal before taking his departure. Old Barry with all his experiences was about as well known as any treasure hunter I could think of. Not even Snude, wild as he was to get at that ore, cared to arouse the man's suspicions by trying to hustle him off.

Time dragged past and still he sat yarning until Serafina, with a glance slanched at Snude, asked if the guest cared to join us in another meal. Storm gave her one of his charming smiles, but reckoned he'd better be on his way.

"Wouldn't aim to be caught in that gut of a cañon once the sun starts to slip out of sight," he said, getting up and fingering the fire agate bola looped under his collar. "Much obliged to you, ma'am. If you're here on a prospect, I'll likely see you again."

"Why not stay overnight and get an early start?" I suggested, ignoring the hard looks I got from the others.

"T'ain't nothin' I'd like better," he chuckled. "Sure been nice gettin' to auger with you fellers, but there's still a heap of miles ahead of me today."

He went over to his horse and tightened the cinch.

In an endeavor to keep him long as I could, I brought up something they were all interested in. "Did I understand you to say we needn't pack up and run on account of that smoke?"

"Well," he said, preparing to mount, "I wouldn't want to say flat out there's nothing to it, but she's been doin' that off and on for a pretty good while. Just somethin' turning over in her bowels, I reckon. Probably quit in a few days."

Once he had gone, Spartokori said as he got to his feet, "You notice after Chuck put that to him, he didn't waste no more time gettin' out of here? From what I've heard, when they start lettin' off steam, anything can happen. I say we better get away from here!"

"And I say," Snude snarled with a venomous look in my direction, "we better start getting that ore out of there!"

Schroeder growled, peering at me like I'd lost half my marbles. "To get any sizable amount of it out is likely to take three-four days, an' you don't know that we've got that much time. By the look. . . ."

"You willing," Snude demanded, "to pass up your share?"

"I didn't say that. All I'm sayin' is goin' into that mountain again right now would be on a par with shovin' your head in a lion's mouth."

"All right," Snude glowered. "If that mountain's going to pop, the longer we wait the less we'll get out. Whatever amount we manage to salvage, those that won't help will dang sure not share!"

"Those that put up their money are entitled to share. That was the understanding," the Greek said belligerently. "You won't catch me going into that tunnel tonight."

"Me, neither," Bob said.

I reckoned it was time for me to put in my oar. "For two shares instead of the one I've got coming, I'll undertake to get out them sacks. You can get the mules almost up to that ledge, so that's where I'll stack 'em. You won't need to go inside. But once I get them out, the rest is up to you."

They stood looking at me, speechless. Schroeder, I guess, was the most surprised. I reckon he had me down for being short on guts. Made me feel good when Serafina cried, "No, Chuck . . . no! Don't you do it!"

She didn't like thinking of me taking such a risk. It really set me up. I took a good look at my lengthening shadow. It was later than I'd thought. I sent a look at Snude. "Cat got your tongue?"

He fished a cigar from his pocket case, bit off the end, and stuck it in his mouth, all the time eyeing me like he suspected he was having his leg pulled. "You serious?"

"Only if I get the two shares I'm askin' for."

Snude's look swept the rest of them, ignoring the girl.

"We can't take it all," Bob said. "We haven't got enough mules."

"We'll have more," Snude said, "when Pepe gets back."

Spartokori regarded me with a new respect in spite of probably guessing what I had up my sleeve. It was he who'd given me this notion when we'd been up at that cave. He said, "It's all right with me if he's fool enough to risk getting trapped in there."

I could see Snude didn't like it but, if the mountain didn't blow, he liked even less leaving all that gold there for someone else to stumble onto. The Greek's remark and attitude, after seeing that smoke, had pretty well convinced him we were going to have an eruption. Storm's hedging remarks had been the final straw. He turned to Schroeder, "How about you?"

Old Poker Face said grudgingly, "All right, let him have 'em."

Bob Cookson nodded.

"Then I'd better get up there," I told them, and picked up a rope to go catch me a horse. I didn't want to be climbing through those rocks after dark.

Saddled up, I led the horse to where our supplies were stacked

111

and got me a pick before swinging aboard, seeing Spartokori grin.

"What's that for?" Snude demanded suspiciously.

"Standard equipment when a man's huntin' treasure . . . ask Storm," I grunted, and headed for the mountain, paying no mind to Serafina's worried face.

Cookson was probably right in thinking it would be stupid to move out all that ore before we had mules enough to pack it away. I didn't know when Quintada was likely to get back with his smugglers and additional transport. It might be another couple days, I thought. Most of my present hustle was nothing but sugar coating to help convince Snude I was on his side in thinking this mountain had just about had it and could blast off any time — which, of course, I didn't believe for a minute. If anyone knew these mountains better than Storm, I sure hadn't heard of him. And Storm, until I had pinned him down, hadn't seen any cause for worry.

The biggest risk in my bid for an extra share had lain with Spartokori and the chance of him spouting off. I'd seen the amusement behind those shrewd dealer's eyes and his mocking grin when I'd reached for the pick. Fortunately he'd kept his guess to himself, or my extra share might not have been agreed to.

I kneed my horse down the trail through the darkening shadows and sent him up the last leg by the new route we'd been using. I got off him less than a hundred feet below the ledge, taking out the fresh torch I'd stuck into my saddlebag.

The entrance to the tunnel was some forty feet higher. I could still see the smoke against the darkening sky. I reckoned in the dim light beneath it they wouldn't know back at camp that instead of the tunnel I'd gone into the cave where Spartokori and I had been poking around while Snude, above, was making his momentous discovery.

With my light playing over it, I couldn't see any change. Moving over to where Bob's tapping with the jimmy had produced the hollow sound, feet firmly planted, I drove the pick at the wall. The point went right on through for what looked to be about three inches, and hung there firmly locked into the rock and totally useless unless I was able to break it loose.

Grabbing a fresh grip on the haft, I tried to shove it upward without success. I attempted to shove it sideways and still couldn't budge it. I could feel the sweat coming out on me. I stared at the exposed metal part of it, furious.

While I was extremely reluctant to go into that tunnel, it began to seem as if I would have to or abandon my chance at that extra share. I got a leg over the haft and hung all my weight on it. With a screech and a clatter the pick came loose in a fall of splintered rock, leaving a jagged ten inch hole through which warmer air came curling around me.

I shone my torch into the hole and yes, by God — *Eureka!* We'd guessed right, Spartokori and I. What I was eyeing was one of those bulging ore-filled sacks! Here was the short cut I'd counted on to earn me that extra share.

Half an hour of swinging that pick and prizing the rock out gave me an opening through which I could lug those sacks, but I still wasn't able to get into the vault because the weight of the sacked ore above and beyond those directly facing me had them so wedged in that they'd become a wall in themselves. So, filled with black thoughts and an increasing impatience, I went back to rock breaking, thinking I might as well be on a chain gang. But a couple of advantages over the boys in striped pants put real muscle into my swings. All I had to do was break up enough sackfuls to get into that chamber, though for five or ten minutes I swung that pick in the full expectation that, as I demolished these sacks, the ones above would come sliding down and take their places.

This didn't happen. They were locked in too tightly. When

this became apparent, I began to make progress. Each crunch of my pick slamming into that ore was like money in the bank, fetching me closer to that extra share. It wasn't easy. At times I thought I'd be at it forever, but at the end of an hour, damned near exhausted and soaked in my sweat, I reeled half blinded across the debris and into the goal of all this exertion, sinking down in a heap, too beat to do anything but gasp.

It must have been at least another ten minutes before I could find enough energy to pick myself up and, still groggy, peer bleary eyed around at the task yet ahead. First I had to muck out the rubble I'd made to get at it. Without a shovel this took another half hour before I had a clear path.

It was while I was sitting there, trying to get up more steam, that I began thinking of my partners in this undertaking. It occurred to me now that a kind of collusion was mixed up in this some place. It was nothing you could really put a finger on but, thinking about it on better acquaintance, I got the unwelcome impression there might be some sort of understanding between Schroeder and Snude and that Quintada had to be somewhere tied into this. If this were so, it left Spartokori, myself, and Cookson the only outsiders, brought into this to provide — what?

An air of legitimacy? Muscle? Additional trigger fingers? Dispensable help? This last possibility appeared the most likely. It was not the sort of thought of which happy dreams are made. Serafina, of course, would be in the same category. The situation had seemed precarious enough before I'd latched onto this. Now we'd need eyes in the backs of our heads. But not, I reckoned, quite yet anyway. Long as we were needed, we'd be reasonably safe.

It was time I began getting those sacks out.

Chapter Thirteen

MORE ABOUT WALZER

Again, it wasn't easy. Those damn' sacks must have weighed a good eighty pounds apiece — probably more. This ore, as I'd seen from the bags I'd demolished getting into the chamber, was in jagged chunks, most of it, awkward to handle in addition to the poundage. Because of the years they had been stacked as we'd found them, the sacks themselves had lost a lot of their strength. They had to be handled with more care than I'd expected.

By the time I'd got twenty moved onto the ledge, I was getting damned sick of it and hunkered on my bootheels to catch my breath. With time out for meals, even working day and night, I was not likely to be done with this till after Quintada returned with his smugglers. Once that bunch got settled in, almost anything could happen and none of it likely to be salubrious.

Grabbing up another sack, I was about to get on with the next ten when the one in my hands came apart in the middle and spewed its contents all over the floor. In my angry disgust I called up a few words I'd forgotten I knew. Savagely kicking this rubble out from underfoot relieved a few of my tensions but did nothing to remind me of the gold I was wasting until I thought of the sackfuls I'd burst through getting in here. I tried to figure out then the relative value each sack might represent. With jewelry rock such as we had here, this ore by the sack must come to somewhere in the neighborhood of three-four thousand dollars!

It was impossible to estimate, or even approximate, the total value of this bonanza since in some of the places around these walls the sacks were stacked four and five deep by eight and ten high. I reckoned they must have had ladders to hoist those upper tiers in place. It occurred to me now that hauling them off down there — or even getting at them — was going to require more than I had with which to work.

Peering about in the light of my torch, it became frustratingly evident neither tools nor ladders had been left in this place. It was while I was considering where that left me that a rumble resembling far-off thunder caught my attention. With my head to one side, every muscle locked, I felt a vibration in the ground beneath my feet and realized this wasn't thunder but something coming from deep inside the mountain.

I stood rooted there, listening, the best part of five minutes in the grip of real fright before, with nothing else happening, I caught up another sackful of ore and went lurching out to the ledge with it, trying to calm myself with Storm's remembered advice. "No cause for alarm," he'd assured us, eyes twinkling. But Storm hadn't felt the damn' ground quivering under him!

I clamped my jaws and by the end of another hour, working against time with the sweat pouring off me, I'd added twelve more sacks to what I'd stacked on the ledge. Leaning against them in the brightening light, I looked up at the smoke still drifting off the crown and wondered if I dared take time out to eat. Thinking of what might be happening underneath me, I looked toward the camp and, discovering no sign of terror, decided I might as well go down. This was back-breaking work and, without replenishing the source of my energy, it was a cinch I'd be pooped in mighty short order. Floundering down to my horse, I hauled myself aboard.

In the early morning sunshine, as I rode into camp, I still hadn't decided how much I should tell or whom should be given my notions regarding the mountain's recent behavior. I wasn't feeling beholden to any of these *hombres* but a little horrendous seasoning, I thought, might help to keep Snude offstride.

They were all round the fire but Cookson who, having finished his chores as stand-in for Quintada, appeared to be headed for it.

"How's it going?" Spartokori called as I dropped out of the saddle.

Aware of Snude's lifted stare, I said with a shrug, "Looks like time's running out. Lots of heat in that chamber. Mountain's grumblin'. Don't take my word for it," I growled as though offended by Schroeder's dour look. "You've only to go up there to see for yourselves."

"I thought," Snude said, "you agreed to get those sacks out . . . ?"

"That's right," I told him. "For an extra share in whatever I got out."

"Then what're you doing down here?" Cookson asked, having come up.

"There's thirty-two sacks sittin' on that ledge waiting to be loaded. I can't move any more without a ladder, and there are no ladders up there. The rest of that bunch has to be moved from the top, and I've already spilled ten tryin' to get at 'em." They all began talking at once until I said: "You want any more, you've got to get me a ladder."

Cookson, with a show of looking around, said: "And where do you suppose . . . ?"

"Not my problem. Reckon you'll have to make one if you want me to fetch the rest of that ore out. Cut a couple of poles, snake 'em up to that ledge, lash on some cross pieces, and I'll get back to work."

With a worried smile Serafina said, "I'll fix you some breakfast."

Seeing the rest of them standing there staring at each other,

117

I added: "It's anyone's guess how much time we got left, but no more ore's coming out of that hole till I have some means of getting up there to move it. If you want to save the sacks I've stacked on that ledge, you better get the mules up there and start loading."

"Be a job for all hands," Spartokori muttered, and headed for the animals, Cookson trailing after him.

Schroeder, chucking a hard look at Snude, said, "You find the trees an' I'll do the choppin'."

The banker, plainly not liking it, nodded. While the others were roping out their horses, he went over to the tarp-covered equipment to dig out an axe.

I got me a panful of refried beans, a fork to get them up with, and sat down by the fire, thanking Serafina for the cup of java she handed me.

"Is it bad up there?"

"Bad enough," I grunted.

"How much of the ore is still where we found it?"

"Most of it," I said through another mouthful. "Have to be moved from the top on down. They're packed in there like bricks in a wall. We've got to have a ladder."

"I hate for you to be in there," she said.

"I'll be all right if my back holds out."

"But you said . . . ?"

"I know. Most of what I said was to keep the rest of them out of there."

"You don't think that mountain . . . ?"

"Storm didn't think so till I tried to pin him down. He knows this country better than anyone."

"But isn't it scary in there?"

"A mite warm," I said, shoveling in another forkful. "Mountain jiggles a little. Guess that probably goes with smoke." I gave her a grin. "Nothing to worry about."

She came and sat down beside me while I finished the beans. "I wish you wouldn't go up there again."

I suppose there were a heap of things I might have said, but with her sitting that close I couldn't think of any. We looked at each other. I don't know what she saw in my eyes; all I could read in hers was anxiety. I said, "I got to get me a stake."

"But you'll have a stake," she protested, "soon as we get this ore back to town."

"Won't be enough unless I can latch onto that extra share."

Cookson, with no great enthusiasm, went past at the head of the mules with their pack saddles on, bound for the mountain.

Spartokori, last in line, paused to say, "You must have worked like hell to get thirty-two sacks out of there, even with that short cut."

"Wasn't easy."

After he'd gone on, Serafina said, "What did he mean? What short cut?"

"I didn't have to use the tunnel." I told her about breaking through the cave wall.

"But how did you know," she asked, astonished, "the room with the ore was behind the cave wall?"

"When we went up there the first time with Snude, while he was discovering that pivoted boulder that blocked off the mine tunnel, Spartokori, Cookson, and I waited down at the cave for him to come back disgusted at wasting his time. Cookson got to tappin' the walls with that jimmy he'd fetched and came onto a place that sounded different from the rest. Then, when you and I went up there the next day with Snude to have a look at that tunnel, followed it downhill, and came into the room with all that sacked ore, I recollected that hollow-sounding place in the cave. After a bit of figuring, I reckoned the cave was on the far side of it."

Her look, turned thoughtful, rummaged my face. I expect she

119

was thinking how smart I was. "So that was the basis for what we regarded as your crazy offer to fetch out the ore for an extra share."

"It was a bit crazy because I might have been wrong. But if I'd guessed right, there wasn't any danger of getting trapped in that tunnel." There was no sense telling her that, if that wall hadn't connected, I'd not have gone on with it. I said: "I better get back up there and give them a hand."

She seemed so admiring I gave her a hug. Then, with her pulled hard against me, her face not three inches from my own, I gave her a kiss. With her arms around my neck, she kissed me back, not once but twice and, arms tightening, kissed me again before pushing me away to step back, startled.

An astounding awareness gripped us both but, when I reached for her again, thoroughly roused and wanting more, she eluded my grasp, backing off to stand breathing jerkily, searching my face. I could see the agitated movement of her breasts and would have cupped them in my reaching hands had she not so hastily stepped away, arms folding across them, watching me like a frightened doe.

Still breathing hard she cried, "Don't go . . . !"

"I have to," I growled, catching up my reins. With boot thrust in stirrup, I swung onto my horse and frustratedly sent him after the mules. Spartokori and Cookson must have moved those mules along at a pretty good clip. They had them standing in a huddle, two already loaded, much nearer the ledge than ever we'd got with horses, by the time I got up there.

It was apparent that Bob had been inside the cave when, glancing at me slanchways both arms around a sack, he said with an elaborate casualness: "See you guessed right about that wall."

The Greek winked. "Too bad you didn't knock a hole in it yourself."

"If I'd fetched a pick instead of that jimmy, I would have."

I could see that extra share I'd maneuvered myself into was not sitting comfortably in Cookson's acquisitive mind. Shrugging, I went inside and stared at those top-most tiers of sacked ore. No matter how I regretted the passing time, there was no getting at them without a ladder. There was no telling how far Snude and Schroeder would have to go to find any growth that was taller than bushes.

Going back outside, I muscled a few sacks down to the mules, then set myself down to wait for the pole hunters. This got me some disgruntled looks from Bob Cookson and an appreciative grin from Spartokori who declared, "Now, if we were as smart as Chuck here, we could be sittin' there smokin' and admirin' the view."

"Wonder," I said, "how many rascals Pepe'll fetch back with him."

"Being they don't wear labels," Spartokori said, "it would only be a guess but, now that you're askin', I'd say anyway six and if we don't look sharp there could be no shares for any of us. Could be dog eat dog before we get done with this."

"Way to handle that bunch," Cookson said, grabbing hold of the twenty-sixth sack "is shoot the first bastard that steps out of line. And make damned sure he's dead," he added, starting toward the mules.

"When you get that stuff down to camp," I called after them, "better cover it with a tarp and stay with it."

"I already thought about that," the Greek grinned.

Left to myself all alone on the mountain, I got to wondering what had brought Storm over to our camp. He was probably just passing and stopped by to shoot the breeze, but in this kind of country with its unhealthy reputation a man hadn't better take anything for granted. Old Barry was known to be a square-shooter. I couldn't believe there'd been any other reason for his visit than friendly interest. Still — he was pretty sharp and there had been Spanish drill bits picked up along the creek — but nothing else had been found since and that was a good while ago. Barry'd been poking round through this labyrinth a good many years and was bound to have some pretty shrewd notions about the Dutchman's mine. I had the impression he believed it to have been located in one of the cañons.

One of the many stories you could hear held that Walzer's plunder came out of a cañon. You could not put much credence in any statements supposedly made by old Jake himself for they'd been repeated time and time again, each repetition refurbished with new material. But this cañon yarn had a few things going for it not found elsewhere.

Among other things, Walzer was said to have mentioned that the mine was in very rugged terrain and on the side of a mountain with the entrance facing west. So, instead of a cañon, it could have been a deep ravine, perhaps actually a gorge. Hidden, it was said, by the contours of the mountain, you had to be almost on top of it in order to see it, and it could not be seen from below.

Across this cañon, whether ravine or gorge, there was supposed to be a cave and, according to this version, below the mine and going horizontally into the slope was a piece of a tunnel said to have been worked by Mexicans. Considerable detail had given this story wide credence. I can't recall how many times I had listened to various versions, but in each the salient features were mentioned and claimed to have been gotten from the Dutchman himself.

To find the mine, you had to commence your search at "the head of a deep, narrow, north-south trending cañon" by the ruins of a stone house. Following this cañon south, you'd see a cave near the base of a bluff and the walls of a roofless stone house where Walzer and a partner lived while working the mine. Continuing south in this cañon, you were to look for a stone face high up on the east wall. Directly across from this lay the entrance to Walzer's fabulous mine. By a lot of folks' thinking this gorge had to be Peter's Cañon.

Twice I'd been lost trying to check this much out before I'd said to hell with it and gone back to prowling Tortilla Mountain. I'd even wriggled into the barren hole where Snude had discovered the pivoted boulder, but all I'd seen was an abandoned shaft.

Getting back to what the Dutchman had supposedly told others, "a tall sharp peak" could be observed to the south. Quite a number of intrepid hunters had figured this to be Weaver's Needle with the mine to the north of it. Others believed it to be Miner's Needle. A few thought it might have been Tortilla Mountain which reared higher than any other peak in the Superstitions, something like four miles northeast of the preferred Weaver's Needle. This is where we were right now with our camp at the base of it.

Nine cañons in the Superstitions run roughly north and south. There is no real cañon that borders Tortilla Mountain, though Peter's Cañon down which we had come to get here is not far away as the crow flies. I could think of no reason for the Dutchman telling anyone anything. Why would he, except deliberately to mislead them?

Which reminded me of Storm's telling us the quakes I'd asked about — the ones believed to have altered a good deal of this region — were before his time, leading one to imagine those disturbances were back in the dark ages when these mountains were born, with dinosaurs and mammoths prowling the swamps and lush vegetation.

The last quake to rip through these mountains was no further back than 1887 of the previous century. While Barry may not have been right here at the time, he was not a spring chicken. I wondered if he remembered how the country had looked in advance of that shaking. What all this boiled down to was you couldn't take anyone's word for anything if it had any connection with buried treasure.

Snude and Schroeder arrived with a pair of twelve-foot poles and a dozen short pieces we fixed in place with carriage bolts, and I returned to my job of getting the ore out. If Snude thought it remarkable when he found I'd broken a door through the cave wall, he said nothing about it within my hearing.

For as long as I was forced to go up and down that swaying ladder, I was slowed up considerably and compelled more often to take time out to get back my strength. On one of these occasions, sprawled out on the stony floor, I must have dozed off. How long I was lost in this blessed oblivion I've no idea. What brought me back to a frightened awareness was the scary feel of the ground shaking under me, accompanied by rumblings deep down inside the mountain.

I went lurching out onto the ledge in a panic, staring wild eyed toward a camp I couldn't see for the dark and the smoke that was everywhere around me, thickened probably by falling ash. Getting down to my near-spooked horse through that clutter of rocks was no small feat. The wonder was that I got there intact. Once in the saddle, I let him pick his own footing, glad he was able. When we came out on the Spanish Trail, I twisted my head for a look toward the crown. All I could see behind the smoke and the ash were bright orange flashes of flame. No rocketing stones, no sign yet of lava.

I was feeling a mite better now, half ashamed of the panic that had driven me out of there. I reckoned it wasn't as bad as I'd thought. Chances were, down in the valley toward which we were heading, they hadn't even felt it. But I was wrong about that.

The camp was in an uproar. I heard the shouts and cursing half a mile away. Schroeder and Snude were yelling at each other across the fire as I piled off my horse. Serafina, hurrying over, caught hold of my arm like she meant never to let go.

"What's goin' on?" I said, peering about.

"Schroeder and Cookson want to get out of here. Snude won't go till they've got more of that ore down."

"Take it easy," I said. "There's nobody leavin' in the face of that shotgun."

It was in Snude's hands, leveled point blank at the two mutineers. All three of them looked ugly.

Snude growled through his teeth: "There isn't any one of you leaving till I give the word!"

I patted her hand where it gripped my arm as Spartokori, staring up at the mountain, grumbled, "Looks to be about over. Just a spasm, I reckon."

Following his gaze I was considerably astonished. No sign of flame. Smoke was gone, too, not a puff of it showing against the wink of the stars.

It was just then that Quintada rode in with his smugglers.

Chapter Fourteen

A KNIFE IN THE DARK

He had five *hombres* with him, four gun-packing Mexicans and a mean-faced Yaqui. Plus two dozen big mules, each with a stack of burlaps lashed to their sawhorse saddles which I was glad to discover. I hardly noticed Schroeder go stomping off into the dark.

I followed Serafina to where a pot of stew bubbled over the built-up fire where she handed me a cup of Arbuckles's best, shoving a pan and a tablespoon into my free fist. Fetching up a smile for Quintada's bunch, she said, "Guess you boys are about half famished. We've got venison stew and you'll find coffee in the pot. No need to play bashful . . . pitch right in." Which they promptly did without further urging.

Three days away from a razor, brush-clawed, and dusty, they were a fierce-looking lot in their chin-strapped Chihuahua hats, appearing equally ready for a fight or a frolic. I heard the biggest ruffian being introduced to Snude as Benito Canello in his crossed bandoleers. I guessed he was every bit as tough as he seemed with that stubble sprouting out of his moon-shaped face.

They were here at Snude's invitation. It was his job to control them, which I'd have given odds was more than he could manage. We would all have to keep our eyes skinned sharp — no two ways about that. Even so, I wondered how many of us would end up as buzzard bait.

Snude, back in Tucson, was no man to shout *boo!* at, but here in this clutter of rock-littered mountains he didn't have the clout of a jackrabbit. I had to hope he understood that. A man so used to being cock of the walk could easily take too much for granted, and I couldn't honestly feel there was one man among us I would care to rely on.

Now that the mountain appeared to have quit its antics, Snude was hell-bent to get the rest of that ore out. I guessed the twenty-six sacks under a tarp here in camp were not going to satisfy anybody. On the other hand, without the help of Quintada's friends, the most we could expect to pack out of this place, according to my best estimate, was forty-eight of these ore-filled sacks, and that meant putting four on each of the mules we'd brought into this country.

I didn't know what yardstick Snude had used in assembling our supplies, but I'd already discovered the burlap sacks he had fetched from town wouldn't more than cover the ore Spartokori and Cookson had already stacked beneath that tarp. Unless we burlaped every sack, we would not even get the stuff out of these mountains.

I told Snude this, and he called Quintada. "How many burlaps did your boys fetch?

"Four for each mule."

"There you are," Snude said like that ended the matter.

"Then most of this ore will have to stay where you found it."

"What the hell are you talking about?"

"Look," I said, pulling him off to one side. "I've checked our supplies. Twenty-four burlaps is all we've got. Pepe says they fetched four sacks apiece for this new batch of mules. Seventy-two sacks is all we can take. Add it up for yourself."

You'd have thought by his scowl I'd called him a name. Abruptly thoughtful, he said, "After we've loaded your seventy-two sacks, how much will be up there?"

"Most of it."

"You mean to say we have more than one hundred and forty-four sacks in that mountain?"

"Nearer two hundred." I let him digest this. "So what do we do about the ones we can't take?"

That had him gasping like a fish out of water. You had to know the old bastard to realize what this was doing to him; it really had him by the throat. "But, but . . . for Chrissake!" he spluttered. "We can't go off and leave all that!"

"We haven't got enough grub to stay here much longer." I grinned at him sourly. "Maybe you can hire that bunch of pet smugglers to come back for it." He didn't care for that, either. I added, "Share the wealth, sort of?" I thought, by God, he was about to cry! "Maybe," I said, "you could get them to bid on it."

What that brought up was about as hateful a look as I'd ever stumbled into.

"Well," I said, "you better make up your mind. The mountain's quiet right now, but whether it's goin' to stay that way is anybody's guess. Can't have your cake and eat it, too. Leave a pair of those smugglers up here to watch it, load the seventy-two sacks, and head for home."

He yelled for Quintada. When Pepe joined us, he explained the situation. Pepe scratched at his jaw. "I don't know. Be a powerful temptation."

"They can't make off with more than a couple sacks," I pointed out. "Got no animals to pack it. All we want is to keep someone else from making off with it. Or jumpin' our claim."

Pepe Quintada was a great deal short of being as stupid as he looked. "Better," he thought, "to leave two of our bunch."

I put it to him bluntly. "You buckin' to be one of them?" When he shook his head negatively, I asked: "Which among us do you reckon will agree to stay after seeing this mountain about to throw up?"

128

That put it in a nut shell, but Snude snapped angrily, "They'll stay if I tell them to."

I said no more, but they could see from my expression what I thought about that.

"You've talked yourself into two shares of this loot. Mean to say you'd refuse if I asked you to stay?"

I was inclined to ask for still another share except I was already some dubious about the likelihood of getting any. I figured we'd all be lucky if this ragtag crew Quintada had brought did not take off with everything we fetched down.

"No," I said, "I'm volunteering to be one of the paid. I think you'd do better to leave three of our outfit, except for the notions that might give Pepe's friends."

Snude's stare rummaged Quintada who threw up his hands. "You told me to fetch them," Pepe insisted. "You knew the kind of men they are. Offer them enough they'll get your gold to Tucson."

"But how much," I said, "is enough?"

Pepe shrugged.

I said to Snude, "They've got you now. You better settle for half or look for trouble. As for who stays with me, I think you'll find Serafina agreeable."

Snude went off with Pepe to haggle with his smugglers.

Looking back toward the fire, I saw Cookson earnestly talking to Serafina and was reminded of having seen this before. I'd never considered myself to be of a jealous nature but could not repress the angry suspicion this sight of them provoked. What the hell was Bob up to?

Gringos like Cookson weren't above playing around with Mexican girls, more especially with pretty ones. Hearing her scornful laugh, I didn't think he would get very far with her — that he could think he might made me feel like hitting him. And I thought to myself I might do it yet if he didn't stay away from her.

He walked away as I started to come over. Then Spartokori came up to me and said, "What do you reckon Snude is figuring to do?"

"Guess he'll head out with the seventy-two sacks, which is all we're equipped to move at the moment."

"Four sacks to each mule," he nodded. "What's he going to do about the rest?"

"Reckon he hopes to come back after it. Leavin' me and the girl here to hold down our equity."

That fetched his brows up. "Surprised you'd stand for it." The way he stood there peering at me, I expect he thought I should be bored for the simples.

"Safer here," I grinned, "than where you'll be going."

Very slowly he nodded with half-shut eyes.

"Thinking to get some cheap labor," I said, "he's backed himself into a corner. Shoutin' won't help. He's got them camped on his shirttail and no way to shake them loose. Pepe will have told them all about Snude's find or he wouldn't have got 'em out here. Snude has outsmarted himself, if you ask me. If he starts any gun play, they're as likely to win as he is."

The Greek was taking it pretty well, I thought. Not a hint on his face of the rage that must be percolating inside him. "Well," he said finally, "half a loaf's better than none. Think they'll settle for that?"

"I can't see them settling for anything less."

Serafina came to stop beside me. She said with a sigh, "They want half the ore."

"Naturally," I nodded. "He'll either agree or they'll take it all."

"Not without some blood being spilled," Spartokori commented. "And you might as well know there's somethin' come loose in your figure. Thirty-six mules can pack a hundred and forty-four of those ore-filled sacks."

I stared at him, startled, refigured it, and swore. "Not quite," I said then. "Got to be put in burlaps. We're short twenty-four."

"So the bulk of what goes will go on their mules." He grinned at me wryly. "How much do you think we'll be leaving up there?"

I said, disgusted, "You better go check."

"Reckon your guess'll be close enough."

"Then I'd say about ninety sacks. Plus I busted up some getting in there."

"Call it a hundred by the time you get those resacked. Make a pretty good haul if you can get away with it." He scrunched up his eyes and took a look at the girl. "You tell Serafina you volunteered her to stay here?"

"No call for that," I said, grabbing my temper. "She's not figuring to help me steal anything."

I could see from his look what he thought about that and could feel the heat creeping over my jaws. "You want the plain truth. I don't think the rest of you will ever see Tucson."

He fetched up a thin smile. "And I guess you don't figure I'll get back to that bluff."

It came over me that this smiling Greek in a different way could be as dangerous as Schroeder. But I was too riled for caution. "I sure don't," and more words poured out before I could stop them. "Was it your knife they buried along with Ben Flake?"

Those near-black eyes raked my face without expression. "If it was," he said, "I don't lack for another," and went off to where Snude stood jawing with Canello.

As I turned to follow, Serafina clutched at my arm. "I think he means to make trouble."

"Two can play at that game." I patted her hand and tagged after him.

"Half." The burly boss smuggler in the crossed bandoleers with a hard grin was adamant. "You give me half and I, Benito

131

Canello, guarantee to get your ore into Tucson, *señor*."

There was nothing Snude could safely do but accept, which he did without grace and, I suspected, plenty of reservations. With a bleak look at me, he said to Quintada, "Take these fellows up to the mine and start loading that ore."

"Not in the dark," Canello interrupted. "We'll go up in the morning when we can see what we're doing."

Again there was nothing Snude could do but quit arguing. He wheeled a stare at Spartokori. "Go up there with Brannigan and help get that ore out onto the ledge."

The Greek showed another of his thin, mocking smiles. "I'm not crawling around through those rocks in the dark. Send Cookson. He's good at that."

Cookson laughed. "I'm a city boy . . . remember? And I don't like snakes."

"I'll go with Chuck," Serafina said, and followed me over to the brush corral and waited by our saddles while I roped out a pair of sure-footed ponies. Then, with fresh torches, we rode off through the Spanish bayonet and saguaros to start our climb up the mountain.

At the ledge she said, "You've stacked so many here now there's not much room to put any more."

"I'll fill the cave," I said as she followed me through it and the gap I had made in the treasure chamber's wall. "That way we'll keep out unwelcome intruders."

"But what if the mountain starts acting up again?"

"I don't reckon that's too likely. If it does, we'll have to climb out through the tunnel." I gave her a reassuring grin. "Probably rest a few days while it works up more steam."

Wedging my torch between a pair of the ore sacks, I went up the ladder and got uneasily to work. Recalling Storm's words and manner, I felt reasonably sure the mountain had gone back to its slumbers, but I was a long way from taking any bets. I couldn't think what the dark had to do with it, but Spartokori less than two hours ago had refused to come up here.

Working steadily, even with having to go up and down that creaking ladder, by the end of four hours packing the sacks through that gap in the wall, I'd got down another twelve and had the cave's entrance pretty well blocked.

I had the cave's outer edge stacked three high and two deep, enough I reckoned to provide some cover and give sufficient warning of anyone attempting to get it. Thinking of the mountain, I knocked off to build up strength.

Serafina sat herself down beside me. With my south paw cradled in both of hers she said, "I can't like this place. There is something about it that makes me uneasy. Can't you feel it?"

"Being cooped up under all this rock. Safe enough, I reckon, when you think of how long it's been since your kinfolks were up her. Didn't even timber that tunnel."

"Just the same, I kind of wish you hadn't blocked the way we came in," she said worriedly.

"I'll fix it," I told her, getting up, "so, if we should want to get out in a hurry, we can."

Going back into the cave, I muscled enough sacks around to give us a passage against the right hand wall that was one sack wide. Picking up another sack, I dropped it into the far end to hamper anyone aiming to come in.

Back with Serafina I lifted off another tier and stacked these back of the others in the cave. Returning I said, "Expect I can get this next batch off without climbing that ladder." I moved it aside.

Where I'd been working, the topmost tier was now no higher than my shoulders and pulling and muscling another row off that stack was easy, comparatively, and considerably faster. After piling these behind the others in the cave, I walked down the narrow passage I'd left and took a look outside in the murky light so familiar in this country just before dawn. I couldn't make out the camp but told Serafina, when I rejoined her, "Snude will have those boys coming up with the mules most anytime now."

I stretched to ease some of the aches from my back and she said, "How many more do you have to move to have enough out there to make full packs for all those mules?"

"Counting what Spartokori and Bob packed down from here, the ones on the ledge, and those in the cave, I think another thirty-two will just about do it."

"I'll be glad when it's finished."

"If I know Snude, it won't be finished till the last sack's out of here."

"Do you think they'll have any trouble with those smugglers?"

"Depends," I said. "I looked for them to make trouble. But, now that Snude has agreed to give them half, there's a pretty good chance they'll make it to town without any hitch . . . if Snude keeps his word and doesn't try to short-change them, and they don't run into an ambush. Pretty hard to keep a thing like this quiet."

"He agreed to give them half. I don't see how he can back out of that."

"Once they get that ore into town, he might figure to thumb his nose at them. It must be gravelling him plenty to knuckle under like that. He'll have to divide his half among the rest of us, which is something else he won't like, though we haven't so much as a scrap of paper to prove our right to any of this."

"I have. I knew his reputation and insisted the bank's attorney draw up a paper setting forth the exact terms under which I came into this. I got a lawyer of my own to look it over, and he told me I will have to be paid my two shares of everything we recover."

"In the laws relating to mines and mining claims, anyone with

134

the discoverer when a discovery is made is held to share in whatever's found," I said, "but there's ways around that, too. I hope your paper's in a good safe place."

Her only answer to that was a nod.

"And now with this deal he's made with Canello, we'll only be getting half of what we expected . . . even if he does keep his word."

For a girl smart enough to have her bank deal examined by an outside lawyer, she seemed remarkably comfortable with our present prospects, saying, "I think there should be enough for everyone."

It was hard to believe, but it occurred to me the mine, to her, no longer held the importance it once had. Something had evidently shoved it out of top place among her priorities.

I said, "An admirable sentiment, but it's been my experience the more a man has, the more he wants. Snude will be squirming around in his head to find some way of cutting his losses. To him a loss is what somebody else gets."

Moving over to the gap I had chopped in the wall, she gasped, "I can hardly breathe in this place! There's something horribly upsetting about being in here. I . . . it seems to get hold of me whenever I'm inside these walls . . . it's like a hand round my throat. . . ."

As I stared at her, astonished, she half ran through the opening into the cave. Listening to the receding sound of her boots, I could not imagine as she rushed down the passage what had got into her. Some sort of foreboding? A premonition? Or was it just the eerie feel of this place which I'd noticed myself? Something emotional, like the fright, perhaps, of those long-gone Peraltas?

Thinking I should have blocked off that tunnel, I followed her out onto the ledge to find her staring down those rock-cluttered slopes in the direction of the camp, now easily seen in the day's

135

brightening light. The mules in a long line behind Cookson were picking their way through the rocks toward our perch, Spartokori, Schroeder, and four of the smugglers following.

Cookson looked, I thought, pretty grim when, after leaving his horse, he climbed up to the ledge. "Some fool last night," he blurted out as he joined us, "put a knife into Canello!"

Serafina's cheeks blanched. "How badly is he hurt?"

"He's dead," Bob said. "No telling what those buggers are apt to do now!"

Chapter Fifteen

HARD TRUTHS

This could be hell with the clapper off! When Flake had been helped into the hereafter, no voice had been raised in his behalf. We were all too glad to be rid of him. But the boss smuggler's death was not likely to be swept under a rug or easily forgotten. There could be repercussions.

"Did you know," Bob said, eyes hard on mine, "this Benito Canello was Pepe's cousin? Pepe thinks Snude killed him."

"Why Snude?"

"Who had more to lose with Canello around?" He paused and after a moment added, "We're goin' to have trouble with those ridge runners. Quintada, too, likely enough. They're all looking wild enough to bend bar iron. And what's bothering them worst is what's going to happen to their half of this ore now that Canello's not here to look after it."

While I stood running all this through my mind, Bob continued, "The Greek's always figured it was Snude who finished Flake."

"He might have shot him," I said, "but I can't see him using a knife on anyone."

"Well, there had to be something pretty ugly between them . . . you saw how Flake acted . . . like he had a real grudge against Snude."

"Yes, but I can't believe Snude would use a knife to be rid of him. Cripes, I expect we all stood to gain if Flake came here to put the finger on Snude. Quintada, for instance. Look at the way Snude has treated him. And now with Canello out of the way, Pepe is bound to speak for those smugglers. I can't help feeling he has a much larger stake in this business than has been so far apparent . . . him and Schroeder both."

"What makes you think so?"

"Any number of things. Among others the fact that Serafina's uncle . . . the one who gave her the map . . . spent his last days with a family of Quintadas who claimed he was killed in a fall from a horse. What do you suppose he was doing on a horse, a man in his eighties using a cane to get around?"

Cookson looked startled. "Where'd you hear that?"

Serafina said, "The Quintadas told me."

Cookson was thoughtful. "You think Pepe's related to them?"

"He denies it," she said. "I don't know what to think. He's always seemed such a meek, inoffensive little man. . . ."

"Yeah." Bob nodded. "He also packs a knife in his boot."

"You ever see a muleteer that didn't have a knife on him some place?" I asked.

Before he could frame an answer, Quintada climbed out of the rocks to come up beside him. "You've heard what happened last night? Those boys are feeling pretty ugly."

And Schroeder, climbing up to us, said, "I wouldn't be in Snude's boots right now for ten of those sacks filled plumb to the brim."

"Snude say anything?"

"Says he's no more guilty than you are."

"Hell! I wasn't even down there!"

"That's what he means, I guess. Come to that," Schroeder said, "can you prove it?"

Serafina said, "I can prove it. Chuck was never out of my sight! He spent the whole night wrestling that ore out because none of the rest of you would go into that hole!"

The four smugglers came up breathing hard from the climb.

138

Uneasily Pepe said, "Reckon we better start getting it loaded," and, grabbing up a sack from those I'd stacked on the ledge, he wrestled it into the burlap one of the smugglers was holding and sent the man down to the mules with it.

"Just a minute," I said. "This'll go a lot quicker, Pepe, if you and one of your friends stay down there with the mules and tend to the packin' as the rest fetch it down."

"Makes sense," he nodded and started off with the next sack.

"How many burlaps have you got here?" I asked, eyeing the pile they'd brought up.

"Ninety-six," Bob Cookson answered. "You got that many ready to go?"

A rumble came out of the cave mouth. The smugglers still with us twisted their heads to stare at the opening.

Bob said nervously, "What the hell was that?"

"You get used to it after a while," I said. "I've got a bunch of them stacked just inside the cave. I'll have the rest pulled out by the time you're ready for them."

The ground shook a couple times under our feet and Bob, peering up at the crown, exclaimed, "Son of a bitch is smokin' again!"

The work went faster after that, none of them wanting to be up here any longer than they had to be. Snude came up to the ledge about an hour later when half the ore I had out there had been carried down, and the mountain let out another rumble to welcome him. When the ground jerked under his feet, the banker looked like he was going to heave up his breakfast.

"Changed my mind," I said, "about us stayin' up here. When the rest of you pull out, we're going along with you."

Snude's brows came down in the start of a scowl. "What about the rest of that ore in there?"

"What about you stayin' up here to see to it?"

Snude's eyes popped open then winnowed down to glittering

139

slits. He looked angry enough to burst a vessel. "God damn it, Chuck, I've been counting on you!"

"Better check your figures."

"I'm giving you two shares!"

"Never mind the shares." I dredged up a scowl of my own. "If you're not fixin' to stay, you'd better go down with those loaded mules, or first thing you know you'll have 'em piled up with a bunch of broken legs!"

He peered after the mules that were on their way with full packs, a couple of smugglers hustling them through that tangle of rocks, very anxious it seemed to get off the mountain.

Twisting around, he jabbed his meanest stare at me. "Right now," he said with hate in his voice, "we're talking about all that ore we can't move, that we're all going to lose if somebody makes off with it!"

"It's been up here ever since it was mined. Who but the Dutchman has ever moved any of it?"

"We've beat a track into this ground you can see two miles off!"

"Only," I said, "if you know where to look. You're puttin' your worry at the wrong end of this. It's the smugglers and Schroeder and that Greek you've got to watch . . . they're the ones who have their eyes on your ore. Them and Pepe Quintada who thinks you put that knife in his cousin!"

The banker's face turned apoplectic, and I thought for a moment he meant to grab hold of me — he looked furious enough to do it. I said, beating him to the punch, "Out here in these mountains you got no clout at all. There's not a man in this bunch who hasn't got it in for you. About time you woke up!"

I could see those hard truths digging into him plenty. I went on, "You're not foolin' any one. The way this shapes up you haven't the ghost of a chance of ever gettin' to Tucson. Scrub out your damn' shares! Give me two out of every five sacks

140

that reach your bank, and I'll undertake to get this ore into town . . . yes, an' you along with it."

Of course, he didn't like it, but he could see where he stood. Without a friend in the camp he didn't have much choice. He hung fire a few seconds trying to see how he could welch once he got back his clout.

"What about the half I had to promise those smugglers?"

"Your deal was with Canello. He won't complain. You put me in charge, I'll take care of everything."

Right then something under that mountain kicked up again. The ground beneath our feet began to quiver.

"By God," he snarled, "I'm going to hold you to it!" He whirled to take off.

"Not so fast," I growled. "I'll want that in writing."

He jerked me a backward stare. "Later," he grumbled over his shoulder.

"Right now," I said, "or you can take your chances."

He almost forgot his fright in his fury.

"Right now," I repeated.

He scribbled in his tally book and tore off the sheet.

"Put your name to it," I told him and, when he did, I said, "Now fetch it up here."

I thought for a second he was going to balk. But the ground quivered again and he came near enough to slap it into my hand before scurrying for his horse.

"Watch out you don't get killed before I get down there."

When he got to where they were holding the mules, he sent Cookson off with the ones that were loaded and snarled at the others to get the rest of them packed. Then set off after Bob.

The mountain burped again, the sound of it like ten tons of slag being dumped down a chute, and the ground began jiggling till I could hardly keep my feet. When it quit, I went inside, warbling like a drunken Indian and got back to work. I sure as hell didn't want to, but I still had thirty-two sacks to muscle out.

Despite Storm's easy assurance, I couldn't help wondering if this could be the time the mountain was going to come apart. I had a damned queasy feeling way down in my innards.

The first ten sacks I pulled off the pile I lugged out through the cave and stacked on the ledge. When I brought out the eleventh, three of the smugglers and Spartokori were moving down through the rocks, each clutching a burlaped sack.

"Be a little careful with them," I called. "That canvas rips easy."

Grunting and cursing, they scrambled on through the rocks. Grimacing, I went back inside.

"You should have told them," Serafina said, "you've been appointed boss of this outfit."

"No sense making them more riled than they already are. I'll let them know when I have to."

"Has the mountain quit smoking?"

"Never noticed. If it hasn't, I expect the wind's carrying it off." I fetched up a tired smile. "Reckon I better get at it again. They've got that ledge almost cleared."

"Why don't you stack what's in the cave back of those others?"

"No, I'll put the rest out there. Only twenty-one more of them to move."

First sack I grabbed up broke apart in my hands. Smothering an oath, I reached for another. By the end of the next hour I'd put another ten out there.

The mountain fetched up a sound like a fast express on the Southern Pacific. The ground shook under us, and Serafina turned pale as a bed sheet.

"Only eleven more to go," I grinned, thinking to cheer her up. "Guess you'll be glad to get out of here."

She showed a wan smile. "I can hardly wait."

"Why don't you come outside?" I said, hugging another sack to my chest, and couldn't help thinking I'd would have liked it better if it had been her in my arms.

She followed me out, and, just as I was lowering my load to the ledge, that bitch of a mountain wrenched up another spasm, damned near throwing me into the rocks. I hung onto my sack till the ground quit shaking.

Eyes enormous, Serafina said, "Doesn't it seem likely to you they're getting closer together?"

Shrugging, I went back to bring out the next sack. I found another pair of sacks had broken apart in that shudder. Eventually the last sack I had to move was out there.

"Let's go," I grunted, and we started down to where we'd left our horses.

Three empty-handed smugglers passed us, scowling, coming up. Spartokori, trailing them, asked, "You got them all out?"

"All that's due to go," I said. "What mules you've got packed we'll take on down with us."

He nodded and went on.

When we reached the mules, Quintada got off the rock he was sitting on to say with a sneer, "Snude tells me you're the boss now. How'd you get so lucky?"

"By guaranteeing to get him and his ore safely back into town."

Pepe showed me his nastiest grin. "Think you can do it?"

"Let's see your knife, *hombre.*"

I thought for a minute he was going to refuse, but in the end he reached down and got it out of his boot.

I said, "Like the one they pulled out of Canello."

"You accusin' . . . ?"

"I'm not accusin' anyone. Yet . . . !"

"That Greek's got one looks just like it." He added in a surly tone, "Must be a dozen in this outfit, all the same kind."

"I wouldn't be surprised. But if anyone else kicks the bucket

143

from a knife wound, you better be ready to jump."

After swapping hard looks with him, I moved off after Serafina and the loaded mules.

She said, "That wasn't very smart, do you think?"

"Probably not," I admitted, "but some way that feller always brings out the worst in me. Won't hurt to stir him up a little."

"You stir up enough of them. . . ."

"Point taken," I muttered, still feeling too ringy to argue it further.

If my earlier suspicions came anywhere near target, Quintada had been under Flake's thumb and might very well have had more than a little to do with the 'accident' that had caught up with Serafina's uncle.

Just as we came onto the old Spanish Trail, there came another of those soul-shaking rumbles and we had all we could do to keep the mules from bolting. By the time we had them in hand again, through the gathering dark the distant gleam of the supper fire could be seen in the camp below us.

Something slammed past my head with the sound of a hornet. A rifle's report jerked me around in the saddle. Only thing in sight that could shelter the sniper was a patch of chaparral about a hundred yards off between us and camp. I put three slugs into it fast as I could lever.

"Watch the mules!" I yelled and, bending low above the neck of my mount, drove him through a hail of blue whistlers. Half way there, two horsemen burst out of the patch of chaparral, streaking hellity-larrup for the valley, but in the opposite direction from where our camp was. I emptied the Winchester and had the grim satisfaction of watching the nearest flop out of his saddle, but the other one, on a faster horse, got so far away in the dark I lost him.

Pulling up by the one I'd hit, I got down to have a look at him. In the light of a cupped match I saw the bullhide chaps.

He was all spraddled out, too dead to skin. One of that shiftless pair of saddle tramps, the thick-set rascal, not the one who'd yanked his horse into the trail ahead of Serafina.

Having abandoned the mules, Serafina came up as I was shoving my boot into stirrup. The pale blob of her face wasn't able, apparently, to discover the downed man's identity.

"Did you recognize him?" Her low voice seemed huskier than usual. "Who is it?"

"Feller we saw with Black Patch."

"Do you think they were after the mules?"

"What else? And where are they? Thought I told you to watch out for them."

"With you riding into that storm of bullets?"

"Never mind," I said, swinging up into leather. "Probably headed for camp." I gave her arm a hard squeeze. "If not, we'll just have to hunt them, I reckon. Can't afford to lose such a valuable cargo."

"Is that all you can think about?"

"Our share of those sacks will come in pretty handy when we get ready to set up our . . . establishment."

I knew she was trying to make out my face and I grinned through the dark at her. "You aren't doubting we'll have one?"

"I don't feel we should tempt fate by talking of it."

"You do want it, don't you?"

But she wouldn't be drawn. Putting spurs to her horse, she set off for camp, and I followed her, wondering if it was Cookson she fancied. He had a lot more to offer, I reckoned, than I had.

Following her down toward the level where they'd set up camp not far from the creek, these rock-ribbed mountains were much in my mind, as was this silence so steeped in the happenings of unremembered yesterdays, a quiet you might think unfamiliar, an intense stillness seldom broken by anything louder than the cry of swooping eagle or a coyote's yammer from some distant ridge.

I felt little remorse for shooting that rascal and wished I'd been able to drop them both. Too many of their kind found haven in this maze of peaks, buttes, and sun-blasted cañons, preying on fools who ventured in here alone. A perilous place with so many parts of it looking like others. Practically waterless save for three creeks, all of them along its eastern flank.

It seemed like we'd never know when or from whom came the tip which had attracted Snude to this particular mountain. It could have been extracted from Serafina's uncle before he'd expired. Who could inform us? Possibly Flake in some conversation had let drop the spark which had ignited the banker's covetous interest. That Snude from the very start had been making for this place I had no longer any doubt. He had shown very little interest in our surroundings prior to the time this mountain had been named. His mind had obviously been full of something else. Even after we'd come into this area and he'd selected our camp site, he'd stayed wrapped in his thoughts until that morning when Cookson, Spartokori, and I had got on our horses to climb these slopes with him.

Spartokori had wanted a look at the cave. This had not interested the banker. Even prior to leaving camp, Snude had demanded to be shown the abandoned mine I had mentioned. After leaving our horses to go climbing through that jumble of rocks, it was Snude who was right on my heels the whole way. It was obvious now that something he'd heard or come across had settled his attention on that one thing.

It was angering to recall that I had been there before and, despite the plain marks of picks on the walls, had crawled back out to do my prospecting elsewhere. This whole business seemed eerily unreal, especially when I went back over the various steps which had fetched us here to those bulging sacks of jewelry rock

146

waiting for Snude to discover and pack them back to the vaults of Beach & Bascomb in what politicians called the "Old Pueblo." It was dead men's gold buried, it began to look like, over a volcano about to throw off its fetters.

I shook my head at this preposterous fancy and switched my thoughts to the man responsible for bringing us here, bald-headed, tight-fisted Snude who would always put his own wants first, compromise where he had to and wriggle out of every concession not nailed down. Very bright in my mind was that cold-jawed face with the gimlet mouth, secretive stares, and domineering ways. A big man certainly, big all over and even bigger in his own view with those great burly shoulders and grasping blunt-fingered hands. In his own world he was a man with almost immeasurable clout.

Again I wondered why, in putting together this venture, he had picked us six to be in on it with him. He'd explained the girl by mentioning her practically useless map, that eight-by-eleven bit of dog-eared yellowed paper which, even if authentic, bore little relation to present topography. It was easy to see why he'd fastened on me, a cowhand prospector who might be assumed to know more than I did about this end of the Superstitions, the only one of us six who'd ever been here before. It might be argued from this he had no idea how to get to this mountain and had been too cagey to ask. If I was right about Schroeder, the German butcher from Globe with the poker face and slate-colored eyes, he'd been roped in for his talent with guns. Snude might think him a kind of insurance.

But why Spartokori, the Greek dealer in artifacts and baubles, a man whose life had been spent in trade? And why Bob Cookson, another conniving merchant? Was it because he'd figured, completely out of their element, they'd be helpless out here? That left Pepe Quintada, the mule-breeding associate of smugglers who, if my suspicions came anywhere near the truth, had been an integral part of this from the start.

My perambulating thoughts now jumped to the exterminator, the unknown remover who had eliminated Flake and Canello and — even possibly — Serafina's uncle, the last of the Peraltas who had mined in this region. The girl hadn't killed them, and neither had I. Of the rest of the outfit the most likely killers, if you ruled out Snude, were Schroeder and Pepe Quintada. Either one of these, I thought, could have murdered those two and done away with Gonzales. Both of them, I felt, had some direct tie-in with Snude and, as a butcher, Schroeder was certainly familiar with knives. And, though I could not see Snude as a man who would use a knife, I was convinced he could and would kill if it suited his purpose. In the peculiar circumstances attendant on those killings it was essential the victims be disposed of quietly. This would effectively eliminate the use of firearms.

Yet, all this thinking hadn't done me any discernible good and, swearing, I blew an exasperated breath. I still wasn't able to put my finger on the killer or figure out with any degree of satisfaction what had aroused Snude's interest in what I had thought of as an empty hole.

I twisted my head for an upward look. There were no flames wreathing the mountain's peak, but the smell of its sulphrous smoke was still strong in my nostrils. Though this might, I conceded, be a remembered stench.

When I came into camp, the mules we'd brought down were all there, packs intact, enjoying the oats someone had put in their nosebags. Serafina had dismounted some time before and was hovering over the fire, probably preparing something to eat.

Snude, plainly edgy, was still on his feet, still among the quick. He hustled over to me as I was tending to my horse.

"Glad you're back," he said in a grudging tone. "Some of these galoots are not at all happy I've named you boss. When are you aiming to get started for town?"

"Soon as the last of those sacks come down."

"You're not waiting for daylight?"

"It'll be near enough by the time they get down here."

"With all the mules loaded what about our supplies?"

"Only supplies we can take are the foodstuffs. We'll parcel them out. They can be packed in our saddlebags."

"How'll we get back to where we came in?"

"You can forget about that. There's a road goes out below Millsite Cañon but, with the tangle of gorges between here and there, you can scrub that, too. We'll go up Peter's Cañon to Tortilla Flat. You've been in that cañon. That's how we got down here. Rough as a cob, a good part of it, but we've got a good road once we reach the flat. Going to take a mite longer . . . more miles I mean . . . than by the way we came in."

"Why don't you talk with those smugglers?"

"No good handing them that kind of advantage."

"Then talk with Pepe. He came in with those mules."

"Well, I might do that."

I put no more trust in Quintada than in his smugglers. But if he claimed we could get the packed mules out the way they came in, I was willing to go along with it. I walked away from Snude, thinking he probably had not had any real notion of what he might find when he'd launched this venture, or he'd have come equipped for it with at least as many mules as we had on hand now. I doubt any of us had imagined we were likely to wind up with a ready-made bonanza. Well — Flake, maybe.

Cookson was over by the fire, standing close to Serafina, trying to slip his arm around her, and it did me good to see her slap his damned face. Walking over there, I said to him, "That all you can find to do?"

"Don't let that boss job go to your head. We're supposed to be partners."

"Stay away from my girl."

"Or?" he said with curled lip.

"Or you may find yourself in need of repairs. If those mules are through eating, get the nosebags off them."

It was plain he was minded to tell me something but apparently thought better of the notion. He turned away without further words.

Serafina, watching him go, shook her head at me.

"That sort of thing won't get you many friends in this outfit."

"I'm not looking for friends. I made a deal with Snude to get this ore into town and. . . ."

"Come on," she said, "let's eat. You can't do much fighting on an empty stomach."

She grinned when she said it, so I grabbed up a pan and reached for a cup.

Chapter Sixteen

STORM

The rest of the mules came down while we were eating. It was only refried beans, but Serafina'd fixed two pans of fluffy biscuits to keep them company, and her java was the best I'd ever tied into.

"Hurry up, boys," she called. "It's better while it's hot."

Soon as I'd swabbed out my pan, I got Quintada aside. "You've a sure hand with mules, Pepe, and I'd like for you to keep on with them. Take all the help you need, but let's get out of these mountains *pronto*."

He eyed me a couple of moments and nodded.

"We'll be taking nothing but the ore and grub, and the grub can be shoved into our saddlebags. Now," I asked, "can we get these critters out by however you fetched that last batch in?"

"Don't see why not. Pretty rough in spots, but they'll make it. If we'd panniers, they could pack double this weight."

"All right. Let's get started. And watch out for trouble."

I looked over the others, then said: "If we all pull together, we'll get out of these mountains. The *patrón* has put me in charge of this outfit. Just keep that in mind, and we'll get along like a pod full of peas. I don't expect trouble but, if any busts loose, I'll damn sure settle it. Any questions?"

When nobody spoke, I said, "Good. We're goin' out the way those mules came in, and you" — I said, jabbing a fist at one of the smugglers — "will lead off at the head of the column."

In scarcely more than ten minutes we were on our way.

Half an hour later the sun poked its face above the crags, and I could see we were pointed south. An hour later, having left the creek, we appeared to be swinging in an easterly direction with the sun in our faces. Mountains showed on both sides of the column but, recognizing no landmarks, I'd no idea where we were. We were still in the Superstitions. This was all I was sure of.

Just short of noon in a south-trending cañon we made a brief stop for Pepe, and one of his smuggler friends passed us all a handful of jerky which we munched while the mules were taking a breather. Inside fifteen minutes we were moving again, still heading more or less south through alternate patches of sunlight and shadows, rocky walls reaching up at both sides of us.

I couldn't put much faith in these smugglers, but the one in the lead seemed to know what he was doing, so with considerable reluctance I kept my mouth shut. If he was leading us into some kind of a trap, there was nothing I could do until this was apparent. The twisty cañon changed direction frequently, very narrow in places, broadening out in others to appear almost a valley. One of these wide places where we stopped to hang nosebags on the mules in the shank of the afternoon must have been nearly a mile across. There was one sunlit peak rearing up off to the east. With three other peaks showing up to the south, it was obvious to me we'd not yet got out of the Superstitions.

We unloaded the mules while one of Pepe's acquaintances managed to get a small fire started. Serafina corralled the big pot and an armful of tins and began making supper.

Spartokori approached me. "You know where we're at?"

I shook my head. "Haven't the faintest. All new country to me. Long as we're moving more or less south, I expect we're not headed for some kind of scalping ground. No doubt these smugglers have been through here before."

"You don't figure they're intending to try taking over?"

"Well," I said, on the end of a sigh, "I wouldn't say that. They might try likely enough, if it suits their convenience, but you'll notice the *patrón* keeps his shotgun in hand."

Since early morning he'd scarcely let it out of his hands.

Spartokori said, "If they're going to spill blood, I wish they'd get at it."

"You in a hurry to meet you Maker?"

The Greek grinned sourly. "No more'n you. It's this waitin' and bein' cooped up in these cañons. . . ."

I looked around for Quintada, saw that he had the nosebags off and, helped by Cookson and three of the smugglers, was watering the animals out of hats.

Serafina banged out a summons on the kettle with her ladle.

"Might as well eat. We can't do much fightin' on a empty stomach," I muttered, giving him the benefit of Serafina's observation.

It was a short meal, soon eaten, corned beef stew again, uncushioned by biscuits. The only thing she'd added was the water. I scrubbed out my pan with sand and dropped it on the pile she'd already cleaned.

Quintada said, walking over to me, "We campin' here?"

"No. We'll pull out soon as you get the mules repacked. Get those friends of yours to give you a hand. They're pretty good packers."

"Yeah. Had plenty of practice, I guess."

In no time at all we were back in our saddles still heading south, still in the cañon with the night all around us, blacker than hell on the stokers' day off. I rode with my rifle across the pommel. I noticed Cookson and Schroeder were doing the same, and Snude had his shotgun clenched in one fist.

I expect we all had plenty to think about. The only sounds were the plodding of hoofs, the screech of saddle leathers, and the tinkle of spur chains, danglers, and rowels, thrown back at us from the cañon walls.

That it would happen I felt sure. The only question was when. I brought up the rear of our strung-out procession, not caring to have Pepe behind me. All through the night I rode cocked for trouble. The moon climbed up and made a patchwork of shadows against the west wall. I felt stiff with tension and still nothing happened to shatter the quiet.

In a sky streaked with gold and purple, the sun peered over the left-hand wall with the disc of the moon palely showing in the west. The tops of two mountains towered over the east wall, still several miles to the south of us. As nearly as I could figure, we had ought to be just about out of them now. By my calculations, I felt reasonably certain the open desert shouldn't be far ahead of us.

Quintada wheeled his horse out of the formation, waiting for me to come up with him. When I did, he said, "These mules could do with another rest. If we're stopping to eat, there's a place up ahead looks good as any."

"How is our water holdin' out?"

"That's what I mean. There's a spring up ahead. Some of the sacks have burst inside of those burlaps. If it's okay with you, it might pay us to stop and have a look at them."

"All right."

He jerked me a nod and rode off toward the head of the line. Ten minutes later, where the cañon widened to be joined by another coming in from the west, the lead mules were stopped for the rest to come up with them. When I drew abreast, Pepe and three others were getting the packs off.

A thicket of desert willows showed green against the eastern earth-and-rock wall and that had to be where the spring was. No other wood was anywhere in sight so any breakfast we got would come from chewing jerky.

Spartokori with two waterbags was headed for the thicket, and

I was thinking of getting my own canteen and Serafina's when something slammed past my head so close every hair on my neck must have stood straight up. Following the whip-like crack of a rifle, the Greek, ahead of me, spun and fell headlong.

Scrunched nerves flung me around on the instant, reaching for leather, eyes raking the shapes of men and mules, unable to pick out the source of that shot. Apparently hoping to show up his *compadres,* someone thinking to garner renown in that moment of confusion by dropping me in advance of their schedule had only succeeded in hitting the wrong man.

"Which of you free-trading bastards fired that rifle?"

Even though bound to intensify their hazards no one, it seemed, was going to point him out. There were several shocked expressions. A couple I took to be furious, but every eye in those gone-still shapes without exception was fixed on me.

I stared back at them grimly, bitterly aware that I would get nothing out of them. I sent Cookson over to see if anything could be done for Spartokori. To the rest I said, "Get your waterbags and canteens filled and get the packs back on those mules. We're movin' out straightaway."

Cookson came back. "All we can do for the Greek is bury him."

With most of the others still eyeing me, it came into my mind that, now we'd been alerted, the mutineers among us might elect at any moment to go on with their intentions and finish this here and now. I stabbed a fist at two of Pepe's friends.

"You two break out shovels and bury that handiwork, and" — I growled when they didn't move — "I mean *pronto!*"

Sullenly the pair moved off to find shovels. Quintada, beckoning a couple of the others, got busy with the mules from which they'd taken the packs. Half an hour later we were moving and, this time, I sent Pepe up in the lead with the threat of shooting the next varmint who even so much as looked like trouble.

Since I had no reputation as a *pistolero* most of them, I reckoned, would take my words as an empty bluff. It was incumbent on me to change their minds, and I braced myself to do it if I had to. A couple of busted knees might work wonders.

All this while, even more than with those smugglers, my thinking was tangled with visions of Schroeder whom I figured was some place mixed up in this. If he wasn't Snude's hatchet man, I reckoned he had to be tied in with Pepe. I had seen those slate-colored eyes speculatively appraising me more than once. To me he had all the gun-slinger's earmarks. More and more it was in my mind it was Schroeder I'd seen by those claim-shack steps back there in Texas.

The next two hours of steady traveling fetched us definitely out of the Superstitions. There was nothing ahead but open desert. We were back in mesquite and greasewood country with occasional patches of wolf's candle raising thorny red-tipped wands. With Quintada at the head of our mule train, we were not about to get within sight of any towns.

Breakfast was missed as we slogged on through the midday, chewing on jerky without dessert. Still plagued by tensions, we made a half-hour stop to rest the mules, cool off our bottoms, and stretch cramped limbs. This was at about two o'clock to judge by the shadows.

I was in a situation that was *muy peligrosa,* to use a phrase frequently heard below the border. I was in a real bind, no getting around it. Hostilities were likely to break loose whenever resentments or plain cupidity pushed these rascals beyond reach of caution. The least lack of heed could find guns blazing, something I had to keep in mind. It was hard on nerves to be continually watchful, not only of Quintada's cronies but even of Snude and the rest of my partners. Whom could I trust aside from Serafina?

I got back on my horse when she came up and we fell in

behind the long string of mules. Out here in open country the others, with plenty of space between them, rode wherever they fancied at either side of the line with Pepe up front as *caporal,* picking the terrain and ostensibly keeping his eyes skinned for interlopers who might have designs on the sacks the mules packed. Since he was picking the route, I wasn't much bothered by the likelihood of those. I had a deal of other problems sniping at my attention. Serafina, too, seemed to have little wish for idle chitchat.

The afternoon shadows grew longer and darker as we jogged along toward still another night on the trail. It occurred to me our Pepe with his mealy-mouthed smiles had been out of our sight on that trek for recruiting a sufficient length of time to have set up an ambush, might even now be leading us into it. The more I turned over this unwelcome notion the more edgy I became.

I had no desire to see us and our ore sucked into a trap. The surest way to combat that predicament was to bring him back and put someone else at the head of the line. Unfortunately, leaving out the smugglers, no one else in this outfit had any idea of where we were. The months I'd put in hunting Walzer's mine had given me a pretty good sense of direction. I hadn't much doubt I could get us into town, but for me to take over Pepe's job as guide would be almost certain to foment trouble and bring on the clash I'd been trying to avoid.

I had gotten myself between a rock and a hard place, and no mistake.

While I was trying to think what to do, Ebbert Snude, that mogul of finance and Machiavellian duplicity, dropped back to have some words with me. Ignoring Serafina, who no longer had anything he wanted, he said in a grudging tone of voice, "Looks like you were right about those smugglers. I'm not even sure we can trust Pepe not to side with them against us. You reckon he's leading us into a trap?"

"It's been on my mind," I told him bluntly.

"What will we do?" He seemed a mite worried. "Think you can get us out of it?"

"I've no idea. Have you talked to Schroeder?"

He stared at me narrowly. "Why him?"

I looked at the shotgun across his saddlebow. No point in telling him my suspicions. "What's he think of you naming me boss?"

He put up a show of puzzled innocence. "What's he got to do with anything?"

"I don't know, but he's the best shot we've got in this outfit. Send him back, and I'll see if we can't cook up something."

He eyed me some more before riding off.

"What was that all about?" Serafina asked, frowning.

"Looks like the *patrón* is gettin' a mite nervous. Worrying about his ore, I reckon."

"Some of it's ours," she spoke up.

"I doubt if he looks at it that way. You have to remember he found it."

Her eyes looked bigger. "You think he'll try to cut us out of . . . ?"

"It's a notion," I said, "that's crossed my mind."

"I've got a paper. . . ."

"Who's going to know that if something happens to you?"

"You'll know it!"

"There's a heap of miles still ahead of us. I could have an accident, too."

She stared at me, sounding stubborn but less sure. "You think he'd dare?"

"Shh. Here comes Schroeder."

Schroeder, swinging in alongside us, said, "Somethin' on your mind, Brannigan?"

"I'm wondering if Quintada figures to lead us into a trap."

Turning it over, he peered at me sharply. "What put that notion into your head?"

"Seems a good possibility. This ore we're packin' represents a lot of cash."

"You think he's in with those smugglers?"

"Fetched 'em, didn't he?"

"On Snude's orders."

"For all we know," I said, "Snude, Pepe, and those Chihuahua bandits could all be in this thing together."

"Old Eb's too smart for that."

"Sometimes these clever ones outsmart themselves. Given the clout he's got and with us out of the way, once that ore's locked up in his bank, he can thumb his nose at Pepe and the others."

He didn't say anything to that for a while. In this silvery light, with the moon half down and hat tugged low, there wasn't any chance of reading his expression. Even in the sun's brightest glare, you could seldom make out what was going on back of those slate-colored eyes.

"Point is," I said, "how can we guard against such a happening?"

"Put someone else up there out front."

"You volunteerin'?"

"I got no more idea where we're at than you have."

He didn't sound much put out, I thought.

I said, "We'd better think of something while we're still able."

"The way to handle this, if you're right in that thinkin', is to start shootin' at the first hint of trouble."

After he'd gone back up the line, Serafina said, "Pretty drastic." The night wind was coming up off the desert, and she pushed a lock of hair back out of her face. "I find it hard to believe he'd have made that remark if he was mixed into it."

"Guess we'll just have to wait and see. Gold can do strange

things to a feller."

It was plain she didn't care much for that. It appeared she felt a sudden shiver.

"All the gold in these mountains isn't worth dying for," she said earnestly.

"Well . . . this breed of misfits generally expect someone else to turn up their toes."

"Oh, Chuck," she cried on an outrush of breath, "why don't we just give it to them?"

"They wouldn't be satisfied with just your share. I can't see the rest of this outfit givin' up anything. Not voluntarily. Besides, like most of their kind, they'd probably shoot us anyway. Not the sort to leave any tongues waggin'."

Then we rode without talk for a considerable distance. It wasn't much sound, but you could hear the slogging hoofs and the faint tinkle of spur rowels as we moved through the awesome quiet of the night. The breeze had gone chasing off somewhere else, and I guessed it was later than I'd imagined.

"But what can we do?" she finally exclaimed.

"Expect I'll think of something," I said with far more conviction than I had any right to feel. She was coming to mean a great deal to me, and I purely wished there was some kind of means for insuring her safety, but nothing I thought of offered much hope. And bullets don't care who the hell they smack into.

I also wished she wasn't riding so close to me. I hadn't much doubt I would be the prime target if we had any trouble with Pepe's longriders. As Spartokori had thoughtfully mentioned, it was anticipation — the god-damn waiting that wound your nerves up tighter than fiddlestrings.

Heavy clouds chased across the face of the moon. This could hardly have had anything to do with it but, due perhaps to some unprecedented atmospheric conditions, we seemed suddenly to have ridden into a vacuum where nothing stirred. I could feel

160

the sweat trickling down my back. My shirt clutched my shoulders distractingly.

Ahead, in the luminous, night-cloaked desert, the mules were approaching a squat huddle of trees, mesquite and ironwood from what I could see of them. We had covered perhaps ten miles, maybe twelve, since burying Spartokori. I was about as jumpy as a new-fledged frog. Heat writhed around me in sweltering waves. Something ripped a jagged streak through the sky.

"Heat lightning," Serafina assured me. "No sign of a storm."

Thunder reverberated off the heels of her words, and rain came down in blinding sheets, slamming into our faces as a wind sprang up in shuddering gusts. The lead mule, snorting, went on after Pepe into the copse, the rest of them following, the flankers struggling in that thorny growth to hold their positions. This I saw in the next lurid flash. Then we, ourselves, were battling our way through the low-hanging branches in what seemed like forever but could hardly have been longer than a handful of seconds. Continuing thunder rolled through firefly lights that were like tiny comets in the murk around us.

The realization came in sickening horror that we were into the trap, that these darting lights were muzzle flashes, and half the thunder was the racket of rifles. There was no telling friend from foe. We burst out of the trees in that downpour of rain, half blinded by it and the wind's buffeting gusts. I tried to catch the girl's bridle, but her horse whirled away. All I could do was to spur after the terrified animal, streaking off like some phantom through the dregs of the night. In this living nightmare I had no chance to look for the mules or anything else, lest in this wild dark I lose track of Serafina.

I pulled up with an oath as common sense returned. I reckoned after a quick calculation she would be all right and would soon be out of the path of stray bullets. The mules and their packs must not be let fall into the hands of Quintada and his Chihuahua ruffians.

Spinning my horse through that sluicing torrent, I kneed him toward those winking lights, reins wrapped round the horn and Winchester lifted in hands that were shaking from the tension that gripped me. With the storm sweeping off in the lash of the wind and nothing between me and them but the drizzle, I picked out the shape of a sombreroed horseman and drove two shots at him, the first going wide but the second wrenching him out of the saddle in a tumbling welter of flailing arms.

Off to the left a muzzle spat flame. I was jounced from my perch as the slug hit my horse. He stumbled. I left the saddle, hit the ground rolling, then jumped to my feet. I still had hold of the rifle. With his shape in my sights, I levered, fired, and saw him collapse across his pitching horse. Both arms clamped to that stretched-out neck, I watched him tear out of view in the diminishing gloom of the day's false dawn.

That soon it was over.

Chapter Seventeen

BACK IN THE SADDLE

The rain had stopped. Having taken stock of our situation, we were just standing there — Snude, Schroeder and I, more or less staring at the things in our minds, when Serafina came riding out of the trees.

"How bad is it?" she inquired, looking round.

"Bad enough," Snude growled.

The way him and Schroeder kept their eyes off each other pretty well confirmed my hunch there was some sort of working arrangement between them.

Sighing, I said, "It could have been worse. We might all have been killed, the stupid way we rode into this. We've lost Cookson and Quintada, if you want to look at it that way, and all the mules."

She said to me, "And the others?"

"Lost two, and I wounded another who was hugging his horse when he got away."

It was anyone's guess who had shot Quintada — could even have been one of his free-trading cronies. They were that kind of people.

Snude, grimly eyeing me, said, "You sound pretty chipper, considering we've just lost our shirts."

"Then we'll just have to find them," I tossed back at him. "After that drenching, hiding their tracks isn't going to be easy. Packed like they are, they'll not get much run out of those critters. We've dumped the biggest part of the worry right smack in their laps."

Snude raised his hat to wipe the sweat off his bald head, grumbling impatiently, "Better get after them."

"I'm ready," Serafina threw back at him, "what are we waiting on?"

"Your cocksure friend who was going to deliver that ore to my bank!"

I grinned at this nastiness and got on the eye-rolling mule left behind by one of the dead smugglers. I led off straight away on the track of our transport. The hoofs of all those heavy-loaded critters had cut a plain trail through the rain-tightened sand.

The biggest question I had to consider was where were they bound — Florence or some hideaway? We would be better off, if we couldn't overtake them, to reach wherever they were heading.

One thing that persistently bothered me was how big was the force with which we had to contend. Now that our rôles were reversed, we had become the hunters, and the advantage, I figured, had switched to our side. In view of Snude's skinflint ways and the smugglers' natural caution, I guessed the high-jackers wouldn't employ more men than they thought were necessary, and already we'd accounted for at least two. Canello also was dead, so there couldn't be many larruping off with our treasure. And one of these was wounded. That made the numbers more equal now than they had ever been.

On our side, too, was the reckless haste of putting those pack-laden mules into a headlong gallop in the hope of losing us. But, if it came to a fight, you could forget about Snude. Schroeder, I reckoned, could go either way. In another bind he might throw in with the high-jackers, depending on where he saw the most profit.

If I could keep Schroeder from defecting, we should be all right, providing those varmints didn't pull another bushwhack.

It came over me wryly there were a sight too many imponderables in this figuring — and not much likelihood of whittling those down.

The trail was plain. We should sight the mules this side of darkness. I told Serafina to keep her eyes peeled.

I didn't like the idea of having Schroeder back of me. I sent a brief glance at him over a shoulder.

"Since your eyes are likely better than mine, how about you ridin' point for a while?"

Out of that expressionless face he said, "I'm comfortable here."

I said, "It's not a case of comfort. Getting back that ore is going to take teamwork. If you're not a team player, now's the time to stand up and be counted."

He cocked that gray glance at Snude and, getting no encouragement, grudgingly sent his horse into the lead. That removed one worry from the many that were nagging at me. I didn't reckon Snude would risk a shot in my direction.

I could see another huddle of mesquites up ahead, just in front of a low hill, but Schroeder, in the lead, gave these a wide detour. Whatever else he might be, he was a long way from foolish. He was no more anxious to stop a bullet than I was. We picked up the tracks the other side of the hill.

With Snude riding back of us, Serafina seemed content to keep her thoughts to herself, and the banker appeared quite willing to stay where he was. He had always been good at looking out for Number One. A real survivor.

We were getting into country that looked about right for an ambush, desert still but freckled in distant yesterdays with clumps of berry-bearing juniper, only the tops of them showing now above six-to-ten foot mounds of sand piled about them by forgotten winds.

Schroeder, looking back at me, growled, "You want I should go around that mess?"

I shook my head. It was already noon judging by the straight-up sun. To swing around that far-reaching stretch of mounds would eat up time we could not well spare.

"Then how about somebody else ridin' point?"

We stared at each other, both mounts still moving, with him twisted around in his saddle and those slate-colored eyes boring into me.

"You don't look like a man who'd be afraid of his shadow," I told him. "Or do you know something the rest of us don't?"

"Why, damn your soul!" he cried, turning ugly. "No squatter's brat . . . !" — and right there he stopped. We both knew why. He said, trying to cover what his rage had betrayed, "Don't you trust me?"

"No," I said.

Only then did he take in the snout of my rifle pointed squarely at his gut. The edge of his tongue swiped across dry lips.

"Get goin'," I told him. "Follow the tracks unless you're minded to finish this now."

He wasn't, of course. Not with that Winchester leveled straight at him.

Still in the lead without further remark — but inwardly seething, I had no doubt, he followed the twisting course of the tracks as they wound their way through those wind-made mounds.

It took a full half hour to put them behind us, and I reckon at least three of us, each time we rounded one scarcely breathing, had both ears cocked for the racket of gunfire. But we came through them safely.

Just as we did, Serafina cried, "The mules! Up ahead! Just dropping over that ridge!"

Why the robbers hadn't thought to waylay us back there I suppose we'll never know. But if they'd spotted us coming out of those mounds, they could be fixing right now to remedy the oversight. Perhaps they hadn't known we were that near

166

to catching them.

"Cut around the ridge," I called to Schroeder.

He said over his shoulder, "If two of us go one way and two another, we'll have 'em in a crossfire."

"Too easy to wind up shootin' each other if we try anything like that. We'll all stay together."

Only a fool would put up an argument with a leveled Winchester ready to drop him at point-blank range. He went forward, riding with considerable care, into what even I thought might well turn out to be another — if belated — ambush.

He rounded the high end of the ridge ahead of me. I heard a panicky shout, cut off by the bark of Schroeder's rifle, and someone else was yelling frantically: "Don't shoot! Don't shoot!"

I spurred my horse forward, saw one of the smugglers writhing on the ground, another toppling from his horse as Schroeder fired again.

"That's enough!" I snarled, coming up with him. The other pair, still mounted, had hands above their heads as far as they could reach.

Snude and a pale-faced Serafina stopped their horses beside me. I saw the mules, packs still on, standing dejectedly a little way off, sweat plainly showing how hard they'd been pushed.

One of the smugglers who had been at our camp, still with empty hands thrust above his head, muttered in my direction, "Damn mules quit on us. We had to give up."

I thought it quite likely they had probably surrendered before Schroeder opened up with that rifle. There was no doubt the mules were bushed. I saw the blood-stained bandage under the open shirt of the fellow I'd shot yesterday and let get away.

Schroeder said cynically, "I can't see the sense of luggin' these bastards back to town. I say shoot 'em and be done with it."

"Oh, no!" Serafina cried. "Let them go. What difference does it make? We've got what we came for. They've been punished enough!"

Snude looked at me. I looked at the two Schroeder had shot, both obviously dead.

"All right," I said to the pair with their hands up. "Go on. Clear out before I change my mind."

They lost no time in making themselves scarce, not even stopping to pick up their artillery.

When the sound of their mules' hoofs had faded, Schroeder said with contempt, "If I see 'em again, I'll make short work of it."

Impatient, Snude said, "Let's be on our way."

"Might as well," I nodded, "if the mules are up to it."

Then, twisting in his saddle to have a last look around, Snude asked in his irascible, carping manner, "What about those two cadavers?"

I said, eyeing Schroeder, "Guess you better have your corpsemaker plant them."

When the banker's fish-belly stare fastened on him, Schroeder with an ugly look got off his horse, went and broke out a shovel. It took him half an hour to get a big enough hole. After booting the two limp bodies into it, the butcher from Globe scooped the dirt back over them, flung the shovel away, and with a furious look at me and my rifle got back on his horse.

Just short of dark we stopped by a willow-lined wash to give the mules whatever rest they could get with their packs still in place. I figured they'd rest considerably better if we got the packs off them but, being in no position to take my eyes off Schroeder, I kept this thought to myself. We let them crop at the trees which weren't hardly bigger than oversize bushes while we chewed up a supper of jerky. Afterwards we watered the mules from our hats.

Desert washes, like this one, were seldom wet. There was not enough water left in our waterbags and canteens to drown a bullfinch. I wondered what we would do when the last of it ran out. Snude was all for riding into the first town we spotted and having the local deputy roust up a few men to make sure we got this ore to the bank.

I said, "We'll soon be needing water, too, but anyone catching a glimpse of this train will know damned well these packs're not filled with Idaho potatoes! Ridin' into any town short of Tucson would be just about as foolish as a man could get. On the other hand we sure won't get to your bank without water and oats. These mules need both. Only way I see of gettin' 'em is to stop at some ranch."

We finally spotted one, pulled into its headquarters not long after sunrise and were gratified to see a big tank dug alongside the windmill. I explained our needs to the square-jawed foreman and he said, looking us over, "Looks like you fellers have got quite a cargo."

"Bullets or cash, I expect we can pay for what we need."

"Where you bound?"

I couldn't see much point in trying to mislead him when, if he was of that disposition, all he'd need do would be to follow our tracks. "Tucson," I told him.

His brows shot up. "Be a couple days' travel." He scratched at his jaw, grunted a time or two and told us, "The water's free . . . help yourselves." — with his glance taking in the gaunted look of our animals — "but the sacks of oats . . . you'll likely need at least four . . . away out here at the back of beyond will cost you double."

Snude fetched out his wallet. He said irascibly, "Name your price."

When the man did, Snude paid him.

We led the mules over to the tank, filling our waterbags and canteens while they wet their whistles. The three visible hands took enough time from their chores to slanch appraising looks at us but went on about their business when Schroeder growled, "Ain't you rannies never seen mules before?"

When I went over to the barn with him, after chousing our animals into the nearest empty corral, the foreman said, "Want us to give you a hand gettin' them packs off?"

"We don't figure," I said, "to be here that long."

With the mules and our horses all fed and discretely watered again, we climbed back into leather and set out once more.

"You reckon," Snude asked, "we'll have trouble with those buggers?"

"I doubt it," I told him, "though we might have to fight off some others before we get where we're going. Guess you know how fast the sight of thirty-six mules all loaded can get around."

Burdened with that happy thought, we lapsed into silence.

The next handful of hours brought us into better country where the cocoa-colored ground sprouted occasional clumps of greening bunchgrass. Snude reluctantly allowed our animals to browse a while. He was in a real lather to get those packs locked up in his bank. I guess, far as that goes, we all were. You might even say the nearer we got to home, the more fidgety we became.

Snude said, "I wish we hadn't stopped at that place."

"Well," I said, "if we hadn't stopped there, we'd have been stranded some place by now. How'd you like to have to bury that ore?"

"You got any idea where we're at?"

"Vaguely. Like that feller said, we've still got more than enough miles to get over. With any kind of luck and riding all night, we ought to reach Tucson sometime tomorrow."

"You mean if somebody else don't come after them packs," Schroeder said, staring off into the lengthening shadows.

"Well, we've got this far," Serafina remarked, "and with any luck at all. . . ."

170

"Knock on wood, or don't say it," Snude snapped.

She peered at him, astonished. "I didn't suppose bankers were superstitious."

"It never pays to tempt Providence. Let's get moving. You take the lead."

We were still heading south by a little bit east according to the stars that always seemed closer when viewed from the desert. The moon hadn't come up, but we could see well enough with no town lights to distract us. If we continued on this tangent, I didn't think we were likely to miss Tucson by more than a couple of stone throws.

About four in the morning we stopped to give the animals another short drink and a small bait of oats. This took about forty minutes. By the time we got going again, the sky beyond the mountain range off to our left was beginning to look a mite lighter as a new day crept toward us. I could see by the way Serafina held to our course she wasn't the city-bred girl I'd supposed.

We rode on through this half light with a breeze kicking up. When I glimpsed mountains ahead and to the right of us and knew by their shapes I was eyeing the Tortolitas, I reckoned we'd be in Tucson or at least at its outskirts some time around noon, if the rivers didn't rise, and we could keep out of trouble.

Chapter Eighteen

THE TORTOLITAS

As those mountains got nearer, I could see I was not the only one who recognized where we were. I was feeling a heap better and pretty set up as I visualized the profits so soon to be divided. My shares might not put me in the mogul class, but they would certainly lift me a considerable way above my former station in life.

I could sense the old arrogance creeping back into Snude with recognition of those mountains. Now that he wasn't more than a whoop and two hollers from reclaiming his old-time clout and authority, I could imagine the little wheels in his think-box churning full tilt as he sorted out ways of eluding his obligations.

I sent a curious glance at Schroeder, still riding in his customary slouch, inscrutably unpredictable as always, the slate-colored eyes in that cold-jawed face staring unreadably straight ahead. I'd have to make up my mind what to do about him now that I knew for certain this was the bugger who had gunned down my mother on the steps of that claim shack all those years ago back there in Texas.

Trigger happy and dangerous as I knew him to be, this was not the same man I had seen that night crouched above his smoking pistol. The same hired killer, but no longer having the same speed and reflexes that had made him such a cold-blooded terror. Nor was I any longer that terrified child. . . .

Flanked by these two, as I jogged along in the sun's fierce glare, I was forced to realize not all the questions I had been plagued with were going to be answered. It was impossible now to learn what secret knowledge had precipitated this venture or taken our outfit to that particular mountain which still gave me the shivers whenever I thought of it. We'd probably never find out if Serafina's uncle had been murdered, or who had killed Ben Flake and the smuggler boss, Canello.

I'd have given long odds there had been some kind of understanding between Quintada, Snude, and Schroeder. I kept remembering it had been the Globe butcher who had first brought up the notion of using Pepe's smuggler friends to help us get that ore back to town.

By ten o'clock we had the Santa Catalinas off to the left of us, and I was wondering what ploy Snude would hit on to bilk me out of my shares. Both Serafina and I had his signed guarantees, but I had to remember that back where he'd come from, behind his desk at Beach & Bascomb's Commercial Bank, this swivel-eyed polecat had a great deal of influence. He might even accuse me of knifing that pair! Inside ten minutes of talking with Snude anyone brighter than a moron would figure, if there was any chance of doing it, Snude would renege. But not this time — if I could help it!

By eleven-thirty we had town in sight. Those oats we'd thrown into them had done a lot toward keeping the mules and our horses moving. We hadn't come in on the Oracle Road but quite a piece west of it, even west of the river, crossing it over the rattling planks of St. Mary's Bridge. Ten minutes later we turned south onto Meyer and on past the grand mansions of the town's upper crust. I kneed my mule up ahead to ride alongside Serafina who turned in her saddle to grin at me mischievously.

"What do you aim to do with your shares?"

"Well," I said, "I'm not planning anything till I get 'em."

"How will you get all your sacks moved out of there?"

"I'm not takin' sacks. I want mine in hard money that's easily spendable. You better do the same."

I figured to know her pretty well by this time, so after thinking a few horse lengths I said flat out, "How would you feel about settin' up house on a ranch of our own? Off the Mammoth Road, maybe?"

There was no pretense about her. With one of those dazzling smiles she said, "I'd like that fine. Oh, Chuck!" she exclaimed, "do you suppose we'll really ever get to do it?"

"I'm countin' on it," I said with an answering grin.

She caught hold of my arm and gave it a squeeze as we pulled up our horses in front of Snude's bank.

All the mules came up with their packs and stopped in a huddle alongside the hitch rack. I slid off my mount, dropping my hand to within a couple inches of my holstered gun as Schroeder and the banker rode up and swung out of their saddles.

"Be right back," Snude muttered, and hurried into the bank.

I saw Schroeder watching me. A number of passers-by had stopped, too, attracted by sight of all those pack-laden mules drawn up in front of the bank.

"I know what you're thinkin'," the ex-gunfighter drawled. "Can't say I blame you. So go ahead, if you're bound to, though I wouldn't advise it. You got your whole life in front of you and a damn' fine girl you hadn't ought to disappoint."

Which was no help at all to my confused state of mind. Maybe he hadn't slowed up as much as I'd reckoned but, damn it to hell, I knew I ought to shoot the bugger, or at least go down trying.

He said, "What I done was a mistake. I've never been able to put it out of my mind. I thought it was your old man coming out of that door. But don't let that stand in your way if you figure you got to have a eye for. . . ."

Serafina, suddenly realizing what was going on, cried, grabbing onto me, "Don't do it, Chuck. Don't do it!"

Well, I couldn't, of course, with her hanging onto my arm.

"You've just saved his life, ma'am," Schroeder told her and, touching his hat, went on into the bank.

I didn't know if I was glad of this interference or not but, before I was able to resolve the matter, Snude came out with three of his employees.

"Wake up, man," he said irascibly. "You going to stand there all day? Get those packs off so these fellows can fetch 'em inside before something happens to 'em!"

With a scowl I got busy. They'd been lashed to the sawhorse saddles. By the time I'd loosened the knots and got about half the packs off, Schroeder came out and pitched in to help. It went a lot faster after that.

When the clerks had gotten two-thirds of them inside, I said to Serafina, "You stay here and watch out for this stuff. I'm goin' to find Snude and see about the division."

Quite a crowd had gathered, watching those sacks going into the bank, curiosity gnawing them something awful.

Snude, with his shotgun, stood just inside the door, his little pig eyes showing a deal of satisfaction at seeing all that jewelry rock being stacked in his vault.

"Why aren't you out there helping?" he growled.

"Guess you've figured by now how much I've got coming. I came in to tell you I'll take mine in cash and so will Serafina."

"We can't do all that in five or ten minutes. I'll set up accounts for both. . . ."

One of the clerks let his sack get away from him. It hit the floor with a crash and broke open. I suppose my jaw must have dropped as far as Snude's. I saw him goggling like he couldn't believe it. The last vestige of color had quit his cheeks.

What had spilled across the floor was nothing but plain old country rocks, not one piece of ore among them. Another clerk, hugging a sack, was picking a careful way through this mess when I grabbed the sack away from him and banged it down beside the other with the same result.

"Come on," I growled at the fellow I'd wrestled it away from. "Let's get a couple of them out of the vault."

We did. Broken open, they had nothing to offer but more of the same. Glaring at me, the words rasping out of Snude's stricken face were of a sort never learned at his mother's knee.

"Well, don't look at me," I said. "There was ore in these sacks when they went down off the mountain. It's those damn' smugglers of yours that pulled this switch! Must have happened after they ran off the mules durin' that fight."

The old skinflint was beside himself. I left him still spluttering, not making much sense, and went back outside, glad to find the butcher had finished getting the sacks off the mules.

He said, "What'd you find out? He try to wiggle out of it now he's got most of the stuff inside?"

"Not yet, anyway. He said he'd open up accounts for us."

Schroeder nodded, said he guessed he'd better make sure one was opened for him, and headed for the door. Soon as it shut behind him, I grabbed up one of the sacks still outside and slammed it down hard enough to break it open. Serafina looked astonished, and even more so when she saw what spilled out of it.

"Come on," I growled, "let's get these mules outa here!"

"But what . . . ?"

"Those god-damned smugglers switched the loads!"

She had her mouth full of questions, but I pushed her toward her horse and got onto my own mule, glad to see most of the crowd had drifted away to spread the news. I could see the headlines:

Snude comes out of the Superstitions with a bunch of mules loaded down with rocks!

"Quick," I snarled, "let's get these mules uptown in a hurry!

176

We're likely to need every one of 'em."

She kept plying me with questions I was too upset to answer. What I most wanted was to hang onto these critters. When we stopped them in front of Steinfeld's Emporium, "Stay with 'em," I said, "I'm goin' to get us some burlaps."

"If we haven't any ore, what's the point in buying burlaps?"

"Not going to buy . . . goin' to charge 'em to Snude!"

When a clerk helped me out with about eight plus a sack of groceries and I'd lashed them onto a pair of those sawhorse saddles, Serafina said: "I wish you'd tell me what you're up to . . . you're surely not thinking of going back to that mountain!"

"I'm goin' after that ore we been high-jacked out of."

"But you don't know what they've done with it."

"I know this much. After running off the mules, they had to be in one hell of a hustle. They had to gain enough time for a chance to bury it. It's got to be somewhere among those mounds. Once he gets his thinkin' cap on, Snude's goin' to come to the same conclusion."

"You can't believe those ruffians will leave it there!"

"Of course they won't, but they'll have to get an outfit together, and they won't have Pepe to do it for 'em. What we've got to do is get there ahead of 'em, and we've got to have time to dig it all up and get under cover."

"Won't Snude have the same problems?"

"You bet. But he's got a heap of clout in this town. He'll be a real drivin' engine once he gets his steam up . . . a regular bat out of Carlsbad! We've got to find grub and enough sacks of oats to last us all the way out there and all the way back to wherever we figure to take that ore."

As we were hazing the mules toward the nearest livery, she flung me another of her worries.

"Snude's going to be awfully angry when he discovers we've taken off with his mules."

"Sure. Mad enough to chew nails, I reckon. Which is another good reason for gettin' a wiggle on. And there's all that ore we left out on the mountain."

She gave me a sure enough horrified look. "You're not going back to that killer mountain . . . ?"

"Nope. *We* are. You want to do this up right, don't you? The only reason we didn't get waylaid in those mounds is they'd already planned to give up when we caught up with 'em and didn't want it to happen there. They wanted to give the wind time enough to conceal their handiwork. They must've known we were gettin' close. With those mules looking about to drop in their tracks, I wouldn't think those buggers had much choice. When they threw up their hands, I was taken in proper. What gripes me worst is knowing how deceitful appearances could be . . . makes me feel like a ninny!"

"Well, you're not alone in that. Not even Snude was as sharp as he thought he was."

Always one to make the very best of a bad situation, as I'd reason to know, this practical side of Serafina's nature never failed to astonish me. I put on a grateful grin but wasn't able to hold it when she said through a sigh, "I'm as anxious to recover what we've lost as you are, but I sure can't see going back to that mountain."

"We have to, while it's still there. Snude and Schroeder will."

"I can see what's in your head. You've got to be plumb crazy, Chuck. There's a curse on that mountain. If we can get back what we lost, that should be enough for anyone. Let the rest go."

"I don't want you marryin' a damned pauper! I'm going to build you the kind of place you can be proud of. When we set up housekeepin', it isn't going to be on any two-bit scale!"

What that got me was a tired grin. It was plain I hadn't much shaken the dread possibilities another trip to that mountain had put into her head. Sure it was dangerous — I'd be a fool not to see that. But the notions I'd been packing around for so long were even harder to dislodge.

Hustling her along, I said, "Look at it this way. That gold's out there just a-waitin' for someone. Wouldn't you sooner it would be us than Snude or those smugglers?"

"Yes, but. . . ." She let out a held breath, twisted round in her saddle to run searching eyes across my face. "I have to remember Snude's out of pocket for practically everything we've used to come up with that treasure, and I can't forget it was Snude who discovered it. Don't you feel he deserves some part of it?"

I reckon I looked considerably astonished, which I sure was.

"While you're rememberin', what about the two hundred bucks apiece the rest of us put up to get into this deal? That, he said, was to buy provisions and our equipment. The agreement was Snude would take care of the transport. The rest of us were to furnish rifles and whatever we rode. I'll tell you this. He was not about to venture into those wilds by himself. He furnished these mules to suck us into this, like his talk of that Dutchman."

"But the mules still belong to him and we're running off with them."

"You bet! It'll take him a while to put together another outfit. Anyhow, he'd already lost them to that bunch of bandits he brought into this. He never recovered them. Spartokori, Cookson, and the rest of us did that. Whatever you think, he never went out there without some tip. Think, Serafina! He found the ore but needed me to show him where it was located."

"You mean he knew that mine was up there?"

"Of course, he knew . . . probably knew all about it except where to look."

It took her a while to digest these home truths. She finally said, as we were shoving the mules through the outskirts of town,

"Taken this way, I don't think that ore will give us much happiness. I wouldn't feel right if we should recover it and do what amounts to thumbing our nose at Snude . . . and there's Schroeder, too. He took the same risks we did, Chuck."

I should have known by now she would have the last word.

"All right," I grumbled, "cut him in then. We'll split it three ways, and Snude can take care of Schroeder out of his third. Is that what you want?"

"Oh, yes!" she said, giving me one of her brightest smiles.

I didn't think much of her view of Snude or that share-the-wealth plan but hoped she was remembering all I'd done for her.

We had put the town behind us now, but we'd been noticed. No way we could have escaped being seen hustling thirty-six unpacked, travel-worn mules out of there. It would be all over town before a cat could scratch her ear. But at least we had transport and, if I'd figured it right, a pretty good lead so far as Snude was concerned.

About those smugglers I wasn't so sure.

I said, "Think you can remember how we came out of those mountains?"

She thought she could, so I sent her up front to break trail. I didn't want her back here in all the dust. If there was going to be trouble, it would come from behind, though I could not honestly see how Snude could put an outfit together — even with all his clout — before tomorrow at the earliest.

Three hours later, after a couple of brief stops, we were into the open desert again, slogging along at a pretty good pace, considerably faster than we'd moved coming in. It was not so much Snude I was worrying about as it was those Chihuahua outlaws Quintada had fetched to help us out with that ore. There seemed a pretty good chance we might have a reunion with them before we were done with this.

180

With the shadows stretching long across the range, we took time out to fortify ourselves with several mouthfuls of jerky while graining the mules and wetting their whistles.

"If you aren't too pooped," I told Serafina, when this had been taken care of, "I'd like to push right along. We'll make better time during the night, and it's a heap less likely we'll be discovered."

"I'm game. There's something to be said for making sure of our share, but do you reckon these animals are up to it?"

"Mules, by and large, are tougher than most horses. One thing we don't want is to get too strung out. We'll travel cavalry fashion in a column of twos and, with both of us up front, I reckon they'll follow. They should be pretty used to us by now, I imagine."

Because it suited me to do so, we gave the mules another half hour to build up their strength before pushing on through the darkening shadows. I figured it would be pretty close to dawn before we reached that ridge this side of which the four smugglers had thrown in their hands.

It turned out to be rather accurate figuring. The coming day was still dark as we came out on the flat just this side of the ridge where Schroeder, before I could stop him, had cut down two of the four who had made off with our transport. The sky to the east was beginning to lighten as I reached out and got hold of the bridle of Serafina's gray mare, effectively bringing the whole shebang to a stop.

It was lucky I did, for in that cessation of movement the muted sound of distant voices came faintly through the surrounding quiet to turn both of us motionless. Someone, it appeared, had gotten here ahead of us.

Softly and carefully, I muttered, "Other side of that ridge."

Though no words were distinguishable, it was plain to me they were being spoken in Spanish, and I thought straightaway of those Chihuahua outlaws Quintada had recruited to help move our ore. Just as swiftly I was convinced the pair I'd turned loose were back with friends to dig up the gold.

Serafina said hardly louder than a whisper, "What are we going to do?"

"You stay here with the mules. I'm going to have a look."

Swinging out of the saddle, pausing only to catch up my Winchester, I headed for the ridge and began a cautious ascent of that brush-covered slope. With the need to be quiet, this was grueling work. Long before I could see anything, I knew I was going to find us badly outnumbered. Just short of the crest I stopped to sleeve the sweat from my face.

There were six of them, I discovered, by peering through the brush. A long trench had been opened between the two nearest mounds. It didn't appear to be hardly deep enough to cover the sacked ore. They seemed to have most of it already loaded. There were fourteen mules. I was glad to see that they were too badly overburdened to do much running.

Stretched flat behind my rifle, I opened fire without compunction. Three of them dropped before they knew what was happening. I dropped one more as he dived for his horse. The other two made it into their saddles and went spurring out of sight. The mules took off, too, but under all that weight the loaded ones soon quit.

Looking back over my shoulder, it was plain Serafina had her hands full. I went tearing down to help her, not wanting the mules to bolt. I needn't have worried. By the time I got down, she had them under control. No waddy I've known could have done half as well. When Snude had fetched her into this, I'd figured her for city bred and was considerably surprised at the way she'd handled those critters. But a moment's reflection did much to convince me this girl I'd teamed up with was a pretty complete hand.

That Peralta blood must have had something to do with how she'd surprised me in so many ways, but I'd scant time to waste digging into it then. It did occur to me that we would be well advised to get out of this region at the earliest possible moment.

The pair that had gotten away now had all the advantage and would likely return for an encore once they got rid of the fright I had given them. We could be in a bad situation if we didn't get out of here before they came back. And we had to transfer a good many of those sacks before we could even consider departing.

We fetched our mules round the ridge and, with both of us pitching in, by the time the sun crept over the eastern flank of the Superstitions, we had our mules packed with four sacks apiece, leaving the outlaws' mules with but three apiece. We had just about finished when Serafina asked, "What about Snude?"

I saw her eyeing that trench with earth heaped at both sides of it.

"Yeah," I said, "better fill that in."

This took another ten minutes of ever diminishing time. Then, with a handful of greasewood stems, I brushed the place clean of tracks while Serafina was moving the mules off a quarter of a mile. After that, by walking backwards, I did the same for the mules of the smuggler. The longer we could keep Snude confused the better, deeming him certain to make for these mounds.

Climbing back in the saddle, hoping he would think he was first to arrive and spend several hours searching through these hummocks, I was scanning the roundabout for sign of the pair who hadn't stayed to be buried when Serafina asked me where we were going.

This was another good question I'd been too busy to think about.

"Big thing right now is to get out of here," I growled. "Let's get these mules moving."

We headed them east into country neither one of us had been through before, while I tried to think where to hide this ore for I sure didn't want to take it back to the mountain. If we'd cleaned out that cache, I might have been tempted. The way things stood, it was out of the question. There were too many rascals in addition to Snude and that gun-quick butcher who knew about the gold still left in the Peraltas' Number Four.

Another notion hit me just about then. Hiding forty-six mules in this kind of country, even briefly during a rest stop, would take a heap of doing!

Chapter Nineteen

A LIGHT THAT FAILED

The idea of hiding this ore a second time and thus freeing the mules for that jaunt to the mountain was of no more use than a .22 cartridge in a double-barreled shotgun. With those two smugglers I'd been unable to drop bound to camp on our shirttails, there was just no way we could manage to disappear or keep these critters hidden long enough to get the packs off.

Leaving a plain trail was obviously unavoidable. Far worse was the fact that in this kind of country the dust thrown up by forty-six mules could be seen for miles. There was no way to get around it. By the same process, expecting to find a large enough cave in those hills ahead of us looked equally futile. The age of miracles was past. Lady Luck seldom favored those most in need.

So what were we to do? There was nothing, of course, but to keep slogging along until that pair of Chihuahua bandits got near enough to put us out of our misery. But wait, two, as I'd already proven, could play at that game! There was nothing to prevent us from setting up an ambush if I could come onto the right terrain. Except I could see she wouldn't like it. She might figure it wasn't sporting!

But I was in no mood to consider the niceties of the matter if it would allow us to be rid of their unwanted surveillance. I believed in fighting fire with fire and had never imagined the meek would inherit anything I'd care to have. The trouble was, of course, that until we reached those hills there wasn't so much as a bush we could get behind to use Indian tactics with that brace of bandits.

About all I could think to do right then was to push those mules along towards the hills and hope the pursuit would keep out of sight till we got into them which, the way things were going, didn't seem very likely.

Looking around at me, Serafina said, "No dust back there. I can't believe they're after us."

"They're after us. There's too much at stake for them not to be. We've got most of the mules and every bit of the ore their *compadres* buried. Besides," I added, "they've a grudge to settle. Their kind set a lot of store by such things."

"I hope you may be wrong."

It was plain from her tone she wasn't putting much faith in the hope, but it was my hope, too, even if a pretty forlorn one. We were nearing those hills now. The closest weren't more than a mile away, and I stepped up the pace about as much as I dared, anxious to get into them before we were spotted.

The sun appeared to be heating up. It could have been just me and the plight with which we were faced. In any case, I seemed to have worked up a considerable sweat. Serafina for her part looked cool enough. She may not have guessed what a bind we were in, but it was plain enough to me that nothing was more immediately important than getting shed of that pair.

Then we were entering a ravine between the two nearest hills, and I said curtly with tension, "Get the mules out of sight and stay with them."

That got me a sharp stare. "Be careful," she said.

She rode off after our transport while I pulled up to scan the miles we had come through, all open country revealing no sign of motion. I had damned little hankering to be tagged by a bullet but spent a long five minutes examining the view without even a dust devil scurrying across it. Then, just as I was starting to turn away, two dark specks emerged at the outermost edge of the terrain from where we had come.

I nudged my mule behind a big rock and peered about for a bush large enough to afford some cover. I discovered a grease-wood I figured would do and left my mount on trailing reins. Seeing the rock as an obvious choice, I got down on my belly and, taking my time to do it, wriggled back of a burro weed so low down and scrawny no one was likely to give it a second glance. Stretched behind this indifferent shelter, I flattened the crown of my hat as much as possible and, rifle in hand, took another good look at those specks.

They were near enough now obviously to be horsebackers. It was almost certainly the pair I was waiting for, though still some miles away by the look. They were playing it cagey, coming along at a walk to keep down the dust.

There wasn't much doubt I would be here a while with that sun beating down on me, hot as a stove lid. Hoping Serafina would have sense enough to remain with the ore, I occupied myself considering the various choices I'd have once those Chihuahuans got within rifle range. All I wanted, really, was to prevent them doing to us what I'd done to their *compadres*. Killing their mounts would take care of that and them too, most likely, forty miles from nowhere. But killing horses or mules was not in my nature. I didn't even need to kill the pair of smugglers. A couple of busted kneecaps would put them out of action in a hurry.

I wished to hell they would get a move on!

Then I got to wondering who had tipped off Snude to that Number Four Mine and why he had done it. It might have been Ben Flake, I reckoned. Serafina's Uncle Gonzales could have let something drop or been persuaded to talk before they killed him. But who had killed Flake and Gonzales? It didn't seem likely I would ever find out now. Scowling at this notion, I dragged my stare away from the riders, and next time I looked where they rode beneath their Pancho Villa hats the specks had grown. Having drawn appreciably nearer, they were not sparing their horses.

With my finger curled about trigger, I waited impatiently.

Then, just as I expected them to come within range, that canny pair, instead of slogging on into the ravine, broke suddenly apart, one dashing off toward the hill at my left, the other swinging wide to climb the opposite slope.

Swearing, with no chance now to knock the both of them west and crooked, I tightened my finger and squeezed off a shot at the one who was nearest and saw him, arms jerking, smashed from the saddle. His erstwhile companion, madly spurring, whisked away through the brush before I could whirl to get him into my sights.

Furious, I sprang off the ground in a dive for my mount. Ears laid back, he tried to sidle out of my reach but, grabbing the reins, I scrambled aboard and nudged him full tilt at the departing shape.

That villain wasn't lingering. By the time we got to where I'd last had sight of him, I couldn't catch so much as a glimpse. Wheeling disgustedly, I dropped my mule back into the ravine and, increasingly frantic, raked his flanks in a hunt for Serafina, only to find that she too had vanished and, worse still, so had the mules.

It was enough to make a parson cuss, but they couldn't have gone far. I'd only to follow their tracks to come up with her. I was also startled to realize that I had put her first, ahead of the ore and the mules that were packing it. I was strangely impressed to discover this change in my priorities — astounded, almost. I couldn't make out when this change had occurred, not that at this point it made much difference. It might have been when we'd kissed . . . !

188

It took the breath of a blue whistler fanning my cheek to jerk me back to more urgent realities. I dug in the spurs, throwing myself forward to get the top half of me as low down as possible. But it was not low enough. My mule hadn't taken three jumps with me trying to scrunch lower when I was nearly knocked loose as something slammed into me with a breathtaking thump.

Nothing but reflexes kept me aboard. It was numbness I felt, and it appeared to be spreading. Through the wind in my ears, I heard the sound of brush breaking. That son of a bitch was after me, and I was in no position for any choice but flight.

We were going all out when pain suddenly clutched me as we tore hard right, quitting the ravine in a mighty effort to put that next hill between ourselves and that devil who was plowing our wake. Rounding my goal, I managed a quick backward glance and there he was, rifle to shoulder, not thirty yards away and gaining at every stride. Circling the hill, I beheld Serafina crouched with blanched cheeks behind her double-action Colt, gray mare alongside her, bunched mules behind.

I knew I was toppling, saw the ground rushing up at me. The last thing I heard as I struck and blacked out was the crack of a rifle.

Chapter Twenty

DIFFERING VIEWPOINTS

The first thing I heard, returning to consciousness and struggling to some grasp of what was about me, was Serafina's jumpy voice, choked with an unbelievable agitation.

"Chuck! Chuck, you've got to come back!"

"Back where?" I muttered, unable to find her in the swirl of pink murk that caused me to wonder if I'd gone plumb blind.

"Here!" she cried in so despairing a tone one could hardly believe it was she I was hearing. "You can't die now. Come back to me, Chuck!"

Could this truly be Serafina, the girl who so coolly had taken everything in stride? I jerked open my eyes, discovering her bent above me, features only inches away, that searching stare great black pools in the sunlit whiteness of her frightened face. It came over me, the softness under my head was her lap. Startled, I made an effort to get up, only to fall back as pain like a dagger lanced through my chest, leaving me limp as a soggy mop.

"Are you hurt?" I growled when I'd got back enough breath.

"No, but you are! Oh, Chuck, before I got to you, I thought for sure you'd been killed. . . ."

"Take a sight more'n that to make me cash in my chips."

"You mighty nearly did! Half an inch higher and you'd be strumming a harp! There are two holes in you. It must have bounced off a rib. I've. . . ."

"What happened to that Chihuahuan?"

"I shot him," she said shortly. "Please try to pay a little attention. I've cleaned both of your wounds as well as I could and closed them both with a poultice of pear leaves to draw out any infection. But you'll have to take things easy. We'll have to stay where we're at. . . ."

"We can't with all this ore on our hands. Look, your intervention was most timely, and I certainly appreciate it, but you must see we can't stay here. We have got to get some place where those packs can be hidden. Snude. . . ."

"He won't know where we are."

"Don't you believe it," I snorted — wishing straight off I hadn't — and, though it cost me something, I got onto my feet. "You can't hide the tracks of this many mules!" I said to her grimly. "We've got to get out of here."

She peered at me angrily. "Do you want to kill yourself?"

"I'll damned sure be killed if we stay here . . . and you along with me."

"They wouldn't dare!"

"If you believe that, you must have lost some of your playing cards. Are you forgetting about Flake and the rest of that outfit?"

It took me a while, but I got back in the saddle. She eyed me in exasperation. I said, "It isn't goin' to kill me to ride a little piece. This is limestone country. There's bound to be caverns . . . caves anyway . . . in some of these hills. All we have to do is find them."

"With the tracks of these mules leading right to the entrance?"

Having no reasonable answer to that, I kept my mouth shut and wished she might do the same. But she didn't, of course.

She said: "How far do you imagine you can stay on that mule without being roped to him?"

"Long as I have to . . . we surely can't stay here."

She said no more, and I didn't either. With her mouth tightly shut in sharp disapproval, she took charge and held our outfit down to a walk. Even so, I'll admit I was plenty uncomfortable

191

and did my best to keep her from knowing it.

I had no cause to worry about getting those packs off the mules should we find a place to lay up for a while. She might appear lean as a whipstaff but, as I'd seen for myself, she could load and unload every bit as well as I could and could throw a diamond hitch with the best of them.

She had a wiry strength and a wealth of stubborn willfulness that had already seen her through situations which would have had the average female scared silly. In the binds we'd run into, she was one in a million. I reckoned I was lucky to have her with me — doubly lucky right now. Imagine her knowing the healing power of pear leaves!

There were times in the next half hour when, between pain and dizziness, I'd all I could do to stay in the saddle. I realized it wasn't doing me much good but, if I fell off, I knew she'd stop the whole works right there and set up camp whether I liked it or not.

There might be more of those Chihuahua *bravos* around or fiddling with the ore we'd left in that old mine's storeroom, but at least we were rid of the ones we knew about. It was mostly Snude who was nagging me now. That two-faced banker wasn't the sort to let grass grow under him. He'd be camped on our trail as soon as he could put an outfit together — and a bigger one this time. It would be just like him to ring in a bunch of sheriff's deputies with some cock-and-bull yarn about Serafina and me making off with his ore. He had clout enough to make it stick if they found us pushing these loaded mules.

With these notions prowling through my mind, you might think I was engaged in some pretty straight convictions, but mostly all I was conscious of was the misery I'd been coupled with, having all I could do to stay on the damned mule.

She said to me presently, "We've passed four hills. There's been no sign of a cave, and you look about ready to bite the dust. If you aim to heal and get back to par. . . ."

"I'd enough of Pa ten years ago!" From a mouth that felt drier than a last year's leaf, I demanded to know how many miles we were from the mine. She peered at me in disgust.

"Can you see those dim peaks?" She raised an arm, pointing. "That's where the Superstitions start, and you know what it's like once we get into them. If you've got as much sense as God gave a sparrow, you'll stop right here."

"We can't stop here with this ore on our hands, Serafina! How many times do I have to repeat that to you?"

With that sun beating down hot enough to fry us where we rode, I saw her mouth tighten up. A resentful flash sprang from her eyes.

"You're out of your head if you figure to fetch this loot back to that mine!"

"Well, I don't. All I want is to find a safe place to leave it. You ought to be able to see. . . ."

"You must want to die, talking like that! I'm as anxious to hang onto this ore as you are but, with the trail we're making, there's no place we can leave it where it won't be found. . . ."

"That's what I've been tryin' to tell you," I grumbled. "If we leave it, we lose it."

"All right. Go ahead and kill yourself!"

She glared at me, and I scowled back. I knew she was right about leaving the sacks. There was no safe place we'd be able to leave them with all these mules milling around, making tracks while she was getting them unloaded. Even if we could manage to cover those tracks, any dirt we used to fill them in would have to be dug and would be at once apparent. We had sure gotten ourselves once more between a rock and a hard place.

I could find no trail around it. The only chance for us I could see was to keep moving and, as though she could track the whirl of my thoughts, she said, "Don't be a fool. Get some

193

rest while you can."

Peering ahead through the shimmering heat, I could see we were almost out of these hills with nothing beyond but open desert between ourselves and those distant peaks. Venturing into there before night put a shroud of darkness across them was more than I cared to contemplate. We could do with the coolness; but the real truth was I'd had about all I could stand of this jolting which I'd mainly endured because I feared that, once off, I'd never get back in the saddle again.

I expect she'd been wondering about that herself. What she had said made a deal of sense. With disgruntled grace I bitterly nodded.

"All right, we'll stop here till dark . . . but no longer."

With that she should have been content, but she wasn't. Any fool could see that. I could almost hear the wheels going around as she searched for ways to override my decision.

She set off to stop the mules while I was endeavoring to climb out of the saddle. It was a tricky business in my condition, and one I was all too aware of, knowing if I fell with a foot in the stirrup, I'd just have to hang there unless I received help. I managed to solve this, half expecting to get kicked, by shaking both legs free of the irons and shoving myself backward off the mule's rump. Fortunately, he ignored such unorthodox treatment. But no sooner had my booted feet hit the ground than I went down like a busted sack.

Doubly embarrassed by not blacking out, silently fuming, I lay as I'd fallen, unwilling to move lest the extent of the damage prove too scary to contemplate and — topping everything else — it would spell the end of everything for which we had hoped.

It could not have been long, though it seemed like forever, before the hurrying thuds of approaching boots heralded Serafina's return. It was then — when attempting to get on to my feet — that I passed out.

When next I was able to take in my surroundings, I was stretched out flat, covered by a blanket with Serafina bending over me. The sun looked just about where I had left it.

"Thank God," she exclaimed in a jumpy whisper, "you've finally come out of it!"

Peering up at her, perplexed, "Out of what?" I grumbled in a tone I could hardly believe came from me.

"The fever," she explained with a hand on my brow.

"You must be thinking about somebody else. I've got no fever. . . ."

"It's what I've just said. You have been out of your mind, pitching and twisting like a snake with its head off."

"Hell's fire, girl. Talk sense! I just got off that mule."

"You fell off that mule three days ago. Now be still. I've just finished dressing those wounds. You'll be glad to know the oozing's quit. They're on their way to healing up nicely, but you've got to take care. . . ."

"Great balls of fire!" I flung off the blanket in a sweat to get up, but stretched out on my back as I was and with her hand on my head, it just wasn't possible. I was held down easily, and I reckoned from that I must be weak as a kitten.

"Quit squirming," she ordered. "You've no need to get up. Another night's rest will be good for what ails you."

Aghast, I stopped struggling, appalled by the thought of all this time wasted. With her hand removed, I came up onto an elbow and, shocked though I was, with a searing pain from my ribs, I dropped back in a pucker.

"Damnation!" I grumbled at her exasperated look. "Can't you get it through your head that Snude by now will be scourin' the hills for us?"

"There's been no sign of Snude, or anybody else. Now, you stay there quiet, while I cook up some supper. . . ."

"We've got to git outa here!"

195

"You behave yourself and tomorrow perhaps. . . ."

Not wanting to hear any more of that guff, I growled through the rest of it, "I'm empty enough to eat a whole horse."

"What you'll get is jackrabbit stew. Be thankful I managed to knock one over."

She flung this back at me tartly as she went out of my sight, leaving me with a new fright to ponder. Rimmed by these hills, the sound of a shot could thump around and about like the bit of an axe. With visions of Snude's outfit arriving any moment, I got myself creakily onto my feet. I peered around for my shell belt and six-shooter and, not finding them, snatched up a rifle that was propped against a rock.

Following this exertion, I was forced to sink quakingly, while the pain settled down, and the dizziness left me. By then she'd discovered I was up and came hotfooting over to give me a scolding.

"Are you hunting a setback? We'll never get away from here if you don't behave."

"Guess again. We're leaving this place just as quick as it's dark," I said with a look that was as riled as her own. "As soon as we eat, you get those mules loaded. We'll be almighty lucky if we've got that much time."

We exchanged hard stares for a handful of heartbeats.

"If," she flung back at me, "you're bound to undo everything I've done, you can pack them yourself."

She folded her arms across the plump bulges that pushed out of her shirt, knowing, of course, with those holes scarcely healed over, I plain couldn't do it.

"That your idea of a Mexican stand-off? Could be I'll surprise you."

She said, hotly furious, "Nothing you do would surprise me by this time. Of all the pigheaded hogs I've known. . . ." and let her breath run out with a sniff of disgust, stomping back to the pot she'd hung over the fire.

Glaring after her, I called: "What'd you do with my six-shooter?"

"I put it under the blanket."

I kicked the blanket aside. Though it hurt me to stoop, I did it anyway. With the shell belt strapped around me, I felt fractionally better, more able to cope if Snude's outfit showed up. Then, having brought Snude to mind, I probed at the queerness of his failure to appear. I'd expected the old skinflint to be hard on our trail long before this.

It come over me suddenly that he'd made straight for the mountain. He might have supposed I wasn't one to leave all that ore without making a push to get my hands on it. He could be there right now, waiting for us to show up.

She must have heard me curse. I saw her head come up as she half turned to look at me. But she didn't say anything, nor did I. I went over to the mule I'd been riding. He looked in pretty good shape — in fact they all did, hardly surprising with three days' rest.

I reckoned I was just getting notional, a hangover maybe from the fever and all, but it seemed to me, as I was gulping my stew, she'd been focusing a deal more of her attention on me than on what we'd come after. I should have found that pleasing, but then I remembered how she came to be in this in the first place and that near useless map which had been Snude's excuse for including her.

This chain of thought made about as much sense as diving through one of Snude's plate-glass windows, and deep down I knew it must have sprung from that fever she'd mentioned. Serafina's undivided loyalty was a thing you could bank on, and these occasional tantrums were nothing more than evidence of strain and a woman's muddled thinking. They seldom looked on things in the manner of men. I figured she'd just get over it.

Having finished eating, I went off to water the animals from the store we'd acquired with the ore-packing mules we'd inherited from the high-jackers. While I was doing this, she was busying herself with tidying up the camp site, dousing the fire, cleaning the stuff we'd used to eat with, and tucking it away in one of the packs.

The several glances I tossed in her direction only strengthened my determination, once this venture was successfully concluded, to get the knot tied as soon as possible, start putting together that ranch we'd decided on, and raising kids who would one day take care of us. I had no business thinking that kind of thing, and I only mention it because that was the trail my thoughts were traveling at the time.

Despite the angry ultimatum she had thrown at me, she was soon putting the packs on the mules I'd already watered. Half an hour short of dark found us heading for the open desert, the mules strung out with Serafina in the lead. I guessed she had come around, as I had, to the reluctant realization there was no place to leave this loot that would be safe from prying eyes.

As generally happens in desert regions, night was upon us pretty nearly as soon as the sun dropped from sight. With this much advantage, I'd have liked to think further of how it would be once we were hitched and snug on our ranch, but the aches left behind by that Mexican's bullet kept getting in the way and more pressing needs had to be thought of — like what would I do if Snude and his new crew had already arrived at the mountain, were dug in and waiting?

What I could do would depend considerably on the layout, the situation, and the circumstances that would greet our arrival. If Snude's outfit turned out to be mostly sheriff's deputies, it would be damned problematical, but I surely wasn't about to pitch in my hand.

With the mules rested up and a good feed of oats in their bellies, we were making good time and, with the night wind cooling us, shrouded by the darkness, we could even have done better — had I not had those wounds and a cracked rib to contend with.

Long before daylight, we were into the Superstitions, the peaks all around us, and slowed to a walk, having to pick our way with great care. The moon had gone half an hour ago, and this only made the dark patches darker. One bit of carelessness, winding through this clutter of rocks, could spell broken legs, and a mule with a broken leg was good for nothing but shooting. The last thing I honed for was to advertise our presence by the sound of gunfire.

We were too strung out — I knew it, and Serafina did — but in this sort of terrain we hadn't any choice. It was the way Quintada and his smugglers had taken getting us out of there and to chance a different route through this labyrinth could easily find us lost.

In this maze plagued by shadows Serafina appeared to know what she was doing, and I could only hope she did. Going out with that crew of cutthroats, I'd been too busy watching for treachery to pay much attention to passing scenery. And thinking about that got me to wondering again whatever had possessed Snude to put any trust in them.

I had to believe Quintada had been tied in with him in some way. There was no other explanation. From Quintada and Snude my mind jumped to Schroeder, that leather-slapping Globe butcher. How much had he known of Snude's intentions? He must have been privy to some part of the banker's plans. Hadn't it been Schroeder who had brought up the notion of using Quintada's connections for getting the ore moved to town? Had they, each of them, been trying to cut out the others? Which of them had shoved his knife in Flake's back? Who had killed

Serafina's Uncle Gonzales? And which of them had done in the boss of the Chihuahua ruffians that Pepe Quintada, with Snude's blessing, had fetched to the mountain to move the loot?

These weren't things to be concerned with now. Hauling the Winchester from under my leg, I reckoned my attention ought to be better employed.

The ground to the left of us was still deep in shadows and, above it, I could pick out a few cold, white stars as we came out of the worst of the rocks to where we no longer needed to watch our every step. Along the eastern horizon a band of faint pink light was opening up behind jagged peaks and, spotting Black Mountain, I guessed before almost you could hawk and spit we would be in sight of our goal.

We were back on the desert floor again and south of us some place was Weaver's Needle. I needed no crystal ball to know it was time to keep our wits about us. Squinting against the increasing light, I could make out the black top half of our destination and was relieved to see no sign of smoke.

Having halted our transport, Serafina on her gray mare was coming back down the line. If she was surprised to find me still in the saddle, despite dire predictions to the contrary, you would never have known it. She wasn't doing any smiling nor was I, being less than an hour from the source of Peralta Mine Number Four.

"What do you intend to do now?"

"I didn't come all this way to twiddle my fingers, Serafina."

"If they're here ahead of us, it may be rough getting into that mine."

"Yes. Just a little." I grinned at her, adding, "Give the lady a cigar."

She was in no mood to appreciate humor. She puffed up her chest, released her breath in a sigh, and bitterly declared, "I can see you're determined to get yourself killed."

I said gruffly, "You knew all along I'd come back for the rest of it."

"We've got the bulk of it on our mules. We don't need any more. Let them have it."

"And divide what we've got with that two-faced swindler? Be sensible. You have a lot more right to that ore than Snude."

"But it was Snude who found it."

"Sure, after I showed him where the mine was. You're forgetting your uncle who fell off a horse? An old man so feeble he had to walk with a cane?"

"We don't know Snude had anything to do with. . . ."

"He knew a damned sight more'n he should have! He didn't put that outfit together on a hunch. I was up there before him, and all I found was the start of a mine that had been given up. You know how he dithered around with no show of interest till somebody mentioned Tortilla Mountain. As soon as he heard that name, he was all git-up-and-go. And the first thing he did, when we camped at the base of it, was insist I show him that empty hole. Doesn't that convince you? He was the first one into it. He found that pivoted boulder, which he wouldn't have done without knowing it was there . . . I doubt there's another man alive who knew about it! . . . unless it was Schroeder."

She said through a frown, "Why him?"

"Somebody had to have wormed it out of your uncle. The only man left who knew anything about it, the last man from your family to get out of these mountains alive. And it's my notion he was killed by either Schroeder or Flake."

She eyed me a while without comment. You could see she was turning this over. "You think Schroeder killed Flake and that smuggler boss?"

"I did right after it happened. Besides being a kill-for-hire *pistolero* . . . you heard him admit shootin' my mother . . . the fellow's a butcher. He's got a shop at Globe. It wouldn't have bothered him any, but I've come to believe he didn't kill either of 'em."

She said incredulously, "You can't think Snude . . . . ?"

"I figured straight off he'd hired it done, which brought me around to Schroeder. But Schroeder, I felt sure, would have gunned them. I couldn't see him using a knife any more than Snude. Cookson, as Sally for our bunch, had plenty of knives, but then I thought of Pepe Quintada who'd plenty of reason to be resentful of Snude. After his quarrel with Flake, he seemed the logical culprit. Then I had to rule out Pepe when I found out the smuggler boss was his uncle. After exhausting the possibilities, I had to come back to Snude who, on the face of things, had to have the most reason."

She said flatly, "I can't believe it," and sat there on her restive mare staring fixedly at nothing I could see. "You must be mistaken, Chuck. I'm sure Schroeder killed Canello. Maybe . . . he killed Flake, too."

"I thought so myself for a long time. But I'll give odds now it was Snude."

"If you say that in Tucson, they'll laugh in your face."

"Probably. He swings a lot of weight behind that desk at Beach and Bascomb's. But somewhere Flake had a part in this business. We're dealin' with a greedy, ruthless man. Flake, with a grievance, couldn't be trusted to keep his mouth shut, so Snude took care of him. Let's get these mules movin'."

Chapter Twenty-One

CAUGHT

She seemed far from satisfied but said no more, as I rode on past to the head of the line. Scattered clumps of long-stemmed grass made fragile splotches of color along the gouged trail left by the mules in our flight from the mountain with this very same ore we were now fetching back. The irony of this did nothing at all toward improving my outlook. Fortune's fool — the story of my life.

Reflecting on this exercise in futility, I felt little different than a horse on a treadmill for all the good I was likely to get out of it. Not that I was about to holler calf rope or pitch in my hand in the grasp of this bitterness. There was gold still up there and, in my frame of mind, I meant to have it whether school kept or not.

Eyes squinting, jaw clamped, I set off for the mountain, the plodding mules behind me, my side damned uncomfortable as we wound our way past slabs of rock rearing up on either hand. Drawing steadily nearer to the goal of all this riding with the crown of our objective frequently in sight, I stared through the glare. I hoped that mountain was resting and would continue to hold still till we were able to get away from it — a second time.

No smoke was visible nor did I see any evidence of Snude in the proximity. However, the fact that no one caught up with us during the days I'd lost racked with fever seemed a pretty sure indication he'd brought his new outfit straight on to the mine. That it still was a mine I hadn't any doubt, with all those stringers of gold showing up in the tunnel.

The Peraltas, alarmed by the Indians, had sacked that ore with the intention of taking off with it but had delayed their departure a mite too long. When worse came to worst, they'd been frightened into leaving it. Someday perhaps, if we didn't leave our bones here, we could open up that mine again — once we had settled with Snude. I'd put away any confidence I'd ever had in him. He meant to claim the whole caboodle. If we bested him here, he'd be after our hides till hell was iced over. He was that sort of galoot.

I was certain he'd be up there, dug in and waiting, and I was willing to wait too, if that's what it took. Then I saw the fresh tracks coming in from the east and so I wasn't surprised, when the camp came in sight, to see the tarp-covered mounds neatly stacked beneath the live oaks. There wasn't a soul in view. I reckoned all of them were up in the mountain.

I told myself no one but a reckless fool would go up there to brace them when, by staying right here with their supplies, we'd have them at a powerful disadvantage. I doubted this would be enough for us to dictate terms with any hope of those terms being accepted, but attempting to come to grips with us they'd at least half the time be in plain sight, coming down that rock-strewn side of the mountain.

It did seem like luck might be turning our way. No mawkish compunctions kept me from considering the fine opportunity I'd have for eliminating a few, possibly enough, to stop them dead in their tracks. It would be like shooting fish.

It was maybe two or three o'clock in the afternoon, so they'd be up there a while, putting those sacks into burlaps, manhandling them out to that ledge below the cave where I'd stacked the others for the trip down to camp. There was time to look about and hunt out a safe cover from which to open hostilities. This close to my objective I was no more anxious to kick the bucket than any of Snude's outfit.

From this vantage point the mine was too far away. Until they came out on that ledge, I'd not be able to get a look at them and, even then, it was going to be difficult to get an accurate estimate, to know how many we had up against us. I could see a huddle of horses and mules but not clearly enough for counting at this angle. The biggest disadvantage that occurred to me was having to let them get half way down before they'd be within shooting range.

"Let's get these mules under cover," I said.

She said, "What are you fixing to do? You're not thinking of going up there, are you?"

"Not right now. Just have to wait and see how this shapes up."

"They're going to have to fetch that ore off the mountain."

"I've had that in mind."

"Well," she said with a searching look, "don't forget you agreed to divide this fairly. . . ."

"Fair's a kind of inexact term. What seems fair to you or to me may not suit them at all. Have you thought about that? Outnumbered like we are, we'll be holding the shortest end of the stick. I shouldn't be surprised if they decided to take it all."

"With those deputies around, Snude wouldn't dare try anything like that."

"A nice thought," I told her. "I admit it's what I reckoned he'd do . . . fetch along some law, claiming we were trying to make off with his ore. In town that would be the slick kind of stunt I'd expect from him. But we're not in town. Right now, I'm betting there isn't a badge among that bunch he's fetched out here."

She turned in her saddle to stare at me sharply.

"It doesn't figure," I said, "two people . . . even drawn to each other like you and I . . . are going to agree all the time about everything. Most things, I've found, will generally work out if you let 'em."

By this time we had all the mules moved under the oaks.

"Let's take 'em back in a ways," I suggested. "We don't want to hobble them. We don't want to lose them, either." I was thinking of the racket I had in mind to make. "If we can find the right place, I'll put a rope around them."

"Are you going to leave the packs on them?"

I shook my head. "Can't roll with the packs on." Scanning the terrain, I said, pointing, "You can dump the packs over there." I'd have liked to use that ore for a barricade, something substantial to ward off blue whistlers but, with me not up to wresting with them, it just wasn't practical. "Best leave the halters on."

I was glad she had more strength than appeared evident. I'd help as much as I could, but with an eye on that mountain side. I got the rope off Serafina's mare and hitched her to my mule. I then bent the rope around enough trees to serve for a corral, leaving both our mounts inside with the others. Then we set to unloading the packs, with me taking it slow and easy.

The job was about two-thirds completed when, taking up my rifle and a pocketful of shells, I went over to the outer edge of the grove and stood alongside a rock, scanning the mountain in the grip of an unaccountable foreboding. The mountain had begun to give off smoke, white and yellow smoke.

To get at us, Snude's outfit would have to come down. With our mules nearly unloaded and busily chewing the tenderest shoots from low-hanging branches, it crossed my mind that the bunch up there could be starting down any time. I took a squint at the sun and could see it would be dark inside of maybe five hours. On that hazardous terrain with heavily-loaded mules, they would certainly be on their way down before sunset, even if we'd been seen — and I was certain they had seen us by now.

It was puzzling, though, that Snude had left no guard with his supplies. If he had done so, it hardly seemed possible we'd not have discovered someone by this time. It kept gnawing at me like the ache in my side.

"Grab up your rifle," I called out to Serafina, "and look around for unwanted guests."

She came back presently to declare she'd not seen anyone within or beyond the farthest limits of the grove. Yet this continued to bother and distract me like a mouse in the woodwork; it wasn't like Snude to have overlooked anything. I could only think that he'd been in such a dither to get the rest of that ore off the mountain he had ignored this basic precaution.

"Keep watch," I muttered, ducking back under interlocking branches, "I'm going to find out what those tarps are hiding. Sing out if there's any change up there."

There was no sacked ore stacked beneath the covers, so I had to assume Snude had not come straight here but had haunted the vicinity of those near-buried junipers until the trench that had been filled in was discovered. If this was true, they would not have gotten here much ahead of us. Perhaps it was this that accounted for his haste to get up there.

However that was, they were up there now. The fresh tracks and these supplies made it practically certain. Having been too late to find the high-jacked ore, Snude meant to make sure of what we'd left at the end of that tunnel. I wondered if he had been around long enough to stake out a claim?

I shook my head at this foolishness. He had possession, why bother? Nor could I picture him being in a listening mood. He hadn't come out here to carve up the profits, no matter what Serafina thought.

Hustling back to rejoin her, peering up at the mountain, I picked out two of them guiding packed mules more than half way down but couldn't recognize either at this distance.

"Stay with the mules," I growled, lifting my Winchester.

She wasn't ready for that and pushed it aside, demanding, "What are you up to?"

"I'm going to give those wallopers something to think about . . . cut down a few while I've got the chance."

"You agreed . . . ?"

"Please, Serafina, put your thinking on what happened to Ben Flake and that smuggler boss. Are you honing to have that catch up with us?"

"I'd sooner lose the whole thing than have any more killing!"

"Get back with the mules before you get hurt. We'll lose it, all right, if you don't dredge up some sense!"

Turning my back on her, I lifted the rifle again and, with the butt against my shoulder, squeezed off a shot that went straight over the rider who was out in front. It wasn't that I missed him intentionally. Possibly it was the light, which was growing increasingly dim because of the smoke pouring out of the mountain. I was jacking a fresh cartridge into the chamber when a pistol was rammed into my back and a voice said: "Drop it."

Chapter Twenty-Two

SNAKE DANCE

Instinct urged me to whirl and take my chances but, with that gun muzzle snubbed against my spine, the smallest motion could be next door to suicide. In my weakened condition with two half-healed holes in my hide already, I wasn't equipped to play host to a third. I let go of the rifle and decided to use reason instead.

"For God's sake, Serafina, do you want to get both of us killed and lose the gold in the bargain?"

"I told you I no longer cared about the gold. The killing has to stop."

Unlike most females of my experience, she had the wit, after that simple statement, to keep her trap shut. I twitched. Then I froze when I heard the double click. She was holding her double-action Colt. The hammer was now all the way back. The slightest pressure on the trigger would cause the pistol to discharge.

Real carefully I slanched an oblique look at her and could tell, the cocked Colt notwithstanding, she was beginning to have second thoughts. Snude's outfit was just about to come in off the trail. I should have known, when the chips were down, she wouldn't stay put! Cold sweat crept through the hairs on my neck. I let go thinking about Snude's men as another notion hit me. Why, in pursuing the gold, had I so often thought more of me *and not of us?* I was muddled enough, and it was my hide of course, but caught up in this question was a parade of forgotten things — overlooked incidents of all kinds jostled their way across the canvas of my mind.

I shook my head angrily, not caring to confront them. It was simple enough, requiring no effort to understand how Snude, when her map proved useless, would have discounted the girl as having nothing more to contribute, dropping her out of his plans like a scrap of waste paper. It made sense of a sort, looked at like that, but incidents suddenly fresh in my mind wouldn't leave it alone. I chucked another, harder look at her, finding her watching me intently. As I stared, a faint smile appeared to cross those red lips which had returned my kiss with such soul-shaking warmth. My throat had gone dry. I couldn't believe she could be such a bitch and was still bogged down in the enormity of it when Schroeder, riding in at the head of the mule team and sizing up the situation, derisively called out, "Fun's over, Brannigan. Good going, Serafina!"

I looked at him resentfully. I had been just a white chip in a no-limit game. It took me a while to get control of my voice.

I said, "And you were the girl who was fed up with killing . . . the viper in my bosom. What happened to that spread we were going to build together?"

"I'm sorry," she murmured. She sounded as if she meant it.

I considered her a while, filled with an unbearable bitterness. At last, as Snude rode in, I said, "Why?"

The gun-slinging butcher from Globe loosed the bark of a laugh as those flat grayish eyes played mockingly over me. "She's Snude's wife, Brannigan."

I watched the snout of Schroeder's pistol come up lazily. It was then that the earth began to tremble. A shot, fired from behind me, hit Schroeder even as he was pitching off his mule to the side.

I was sent sprawling and clutched at the small stones near my hands, as the earth continued to convulse and shudder. The mules were braying in terror and pulling at their tethers.

210

Then, as suddenly as it had begun, it stopped. I was too dazed to do very much. I could see Schroeder in front of me, where he had fallen. Blood was pooling from under him now in a small, reddish web. Snude was busy for a time quieting the mules.

"Are they both dead, Serafina?" I heard his voice asking above me, when finally he approached.

"Schroeder is, but not Chuck." Her voice was very quiet.

I doubted that she was holding that Colt on me any more, but something told me I had best just continue to stay where I was. I could hear Snude advancing closer and then I saw his dusty boots standing about six feet in front of me.

"We've got to finish him, Sera. We don't want a witness. Besides, I really think that mountain is about to blow."

There was once more the sound of a double click behind me.

"No, Eb, neither of us is going anywhere nor doing anything until Chuck has ridden out of here."

"Sera, are you mad?"

"No," she said with a sigh, "just weary of the killing. It stops here. If you try to hurt him any more than he is already hurt, I will kill you. You of all people know I am capable of it."

"Sera!" he exclaimed and then fell silent.

"Can you stand up, Chuck?" she asked.

With pain and some difficulty, I made it slowly to my feet. The smoke was now hanging heavily in the air. It obscured much of the face of the mountain in the failing light.

"When you sent me to scout the camp," Serafina said, holding the Colt steadily, aimed at her husband, "I put your mule outside the rope corral. I know you can still ride. I left your canteen on the saddle."

"Serafina . . . ," I began.

There were tears on her cheeks and her eyes, so deep and dark, were dim in the murky light.

"I am giving you your life, Chuck," she said. "Take it and

211

leave. Now!"

"Sera, you must be mad," Snude rasped. "I tell you that mountain's going to blow. That earthquake was for real."

I felt like a horse with the blind staggers as I limped off toward where Serafina had left my mule. It took me two tries before I was finally mounted. I couldn't help wondering how Snude and Serafina, without even Schroeder to help them, could possibly hope to herd all those mules with their packs and get away from the mountain. My brain must have been as murky as the air had become. I was still thinking about the gold and forgetting that it didn't matter any more to Serafina. Maybe even life didn't matter any more to her. It still did to me, which is why, without looking back, I urged my mule forward and rode out of there.

We had gone perhaps two or three miles. The sun had nearly set behind the peaks and darkness was closing in all around us. The air became less murky with smoke as we increased our distance from the mountain. We had started into a deep cañon, the stone walls towering high above us, the light nearly gone, when I knew I would have to dismount and lead the mule on foot. It was painful getting off, but at least I did it on the first try. My feet were on the stone floor of the cañon, and I was leaning my head against the saddle, taking a short breather. Long ago I had been told a man never hears the bullet that ends him, and it was that way with me when the explosion came.

The force of it was felt long before I heard anything. It slammed the mule onto the left side of the narrow cañon and me along with it. Then came the ear-splitting crash of detonation. The aftershocks again slammed us against the wall of the cañon. My mule was braying in terror. I still had the reins in my left hand and that mule dragged me forward, deeper into the cañon. This went on for some time. There was darkness everywhere. I was covered by what felt like sticky, heavy, hot snow that did not melt upon contact, drifting as a blanket down into that cañon.

I began coughing and found it difficult to breathe. The mule by this time was snorting and wheezing. Finally he stopped moving and just stood there, trembling, probably focused like I was on just getting enough air to breathe.

It was the canteen that saved us. I untied my bandanna, wet it in the dark from the canteen, and wrapped it around my face so it covered my nose and mouth. Then I tore off my shirt, wetted it, and tied it around the mule's muzzle. After that, with me holding onto the reins again, I led the way slowly, very slowly, forward. Frequently we had to pause to rest. I wet the bandanna and the shirt at least twice more that I can remember. Generally, there's no critter more stupid and obstinate than a mule, but this one had sense enough not to fight off that wet shirt. If he had, we probably wouldn't have made it.

By the gray light of morning, I could see that what had been falling over the trail wasn't snow at all, but a kind of viscid ash that must have come from that mountain when it blew its top. We were three days on the trail, the last one without any water whatsoever, before we made it to that ranch where we'd all stopped before. The square-jawed foreman was a mite friendlier this time, obviously seeing that I was about finished from my wounds and lack of water. I ended up staying there in the bunkhouse for three days before I was ready, and the mule was ready, for the final push into Tucson.

That foreman, whose name was Bob Coburn, knew about the volcano erupting, but I was in no position to provide him with any details. Hell, I hadn't really seen anything, being in that narrow and dark cañon when the explosion came. There was no question but this circumstance alone was what had saved my life.

Nothing was ever heard of Ebbert Snude and his wife, Serafina *née* Peralta. As much as I disliked the old skinflint, for Serafina's sake, when I think back on it, I want to believe that somehow

213

they made it out of there and are living now somewhere in luxury. If this were not a true story, I could tie up all the loose ends. As it is, I do not know who killed Serafina's uncle. If I eliminate Snude as being a man who would not resort to use of a knife and agree with Serafina that Schroeder killed Canello, the answer I come up with as to who might have killed Flake is one I do not like to contemplate. And, since I have been speculating all along, and still speculate about Serafina occasionally, I like to think, if I had turned that mule train toward Mexico rather than heading back to the mine, our lives would have been different, and we might be living happily today on a little ranch in Sonora.

I haven't been back to the mountain since I left it late that day. Barry Storm has been, though, and he says the whole area was totally devastated by the eruption. Nothing is quite the same, no tunnel, no mine. He also admits now that he was wrong about there being no active volcanoes in the Superstitions.

I did go back to collect that small cache of treasure Bob Cookson and I had discovered. It gave me a start in the business of raising mules. Other than that, I haven't prospected any more, nor has the urge ever come again.

Being on the board of directors of Beach & Bascomb's Commercial Bank, I get to see the oil painting of Ebbert Snude that hangs in the board room every time there's a meeting. Were I ever to get the urge to prospect for gold, all I'd do is go and look at that portrait. The memory of Snude, more even than of Snude's caravan, would be enough to discourage me.

The only good memories I have of that prospect are of the days and nights when Serafina and I were in love. When I think of them, I find myself whispering a prayer for her — and for me.

"*Vaya con Dios,* Serafina . . . *siempre.*" Go with God, Serafina — always.

ABOUT THE AUTHOR

Nelson C. Nye was born in Chicago, Illinois. He was educated in schools in Ohio and Massachusetts and attended the Cincinnati Art Academy. His early journalism experience was writing publicity releases and book reviews for the *Cincinnati Times-Star* and the *Buffalo Evening News*. In 1935 he began working as a ranch hand in Texas and California and became an expert on breeding quarter horses on his own ranch outside Tucson, Arizona. Much of this love for horses can be found in exceptional novels like *Wild Horse Shorty* and *Blood of Kings*. He published his first Western short story in *Thrilling Western* and his first Western novel in 1936. He continued from then on to write prolifically, both under his own name and the bylines Drake C. Denver and Clem Colt. During the Second World War, he served with the U. S. Army Field Artillery. In 1949-1952 he worked as horse editor for *Texas Livestock Journal*. He was one of the founding members of the Western Writers of America in 1953 and served twice as its president. His first Golden Spur Award from the Western Writers of America came to him for best Western reviewer and critic in 1954. In 1958-1962 he was frontier fiction reviewer for the *New York Times Book Review*. His second Golden Spur came for his novel, *Long Run*. His virtues as an author of Western fiction include a tremendous sense of authenticity, an ability to keep the pace of a story from ever lagging, and a fecund inventiveness for plot twists and situations. Some of his finest novels have had off-trail protagonists such as *The*

Barber of Tubac, while both *Not Grass Alone* and *Strawberry Roan* are notable for their outstanding female characters. His books have sold over 50,000,000 copies worldwide and have been translated into the principal European languages. *The Los Angeles Times* once praised him for his "marvelous lingo, salty humor, and real characters." Above all, a Western story by Nelson C. Nye possesses a vital energy that is both propulsive and persuasive. *The Man from Wells Fargo* is his next Five Star Western.